THE LUCKY COIN

& OTHER STORIES

S P SINGH

AUTHOR OF PARROT UNDER THE PINE TREE

Invincible Publishers

First published in India in 2018

ISBN: 978-93-88333-27-6

Invincible Publishers

G-120, Sushant Lok III, Sector 57, Gurgaon-122002

Registered Address: Opposite Kasturba Ashram,
Radaur, Haryana–135133

In loving memory
of
my parents

DISCLAIMER

These stories are the works of fiction. The names, places, characters and incidents portrayed in them are the works of author's imagination. Any resemblance to the actual persons, living or dead, events or localities, is purely coincidental.

CONTENTS

ACKNOWLEDGEMENTS

I wish to express my deep sense of gratitude to the places, mentioned in the book, for inspiring me to write these stories.

My sincere thanks to Ashish Samant for designing the book cover, Ruchika Khanna for the design and layout of the book interior, Rashmi Singh for editing the manuscript, and Ajay Setia for his passionate efforts in making the book available to the readers.

Finally, a big 'Thank You' to Robert Wratz, Minnesota, USA for reading my books and sharing his generous and inspiring reviews with book lovers on the social media.

The Lucky Coin

Ramakant Chaturvedi was a quintessential middle class, struggling, unemployed, thirty-three year old man. After graduating from Sanskrit University in Varanasi he had applied for jobs in various institutions and colleges, but without any success. Time was running out for him as he had only a couple of years left to try for the government jobs for which the age limit for an upper caste candidate was thirty-five years. Unlike the backward and SC/ST candidates, he didn't have the luxury of relaxation in the age.

In the post-Mandal India, the jobs for the jobless like him were rare and people with right political connections or capacity to pay huge bribes only could get the jobs. The unemployed youth roamed the city streets wasting their time at the tea stalls and the paan shops.

Dinanath Chaturvedi, his father, was a high school teacher. In addition to his job, he conducted the puja during the marriage, birth, death and on other important occasions. He was in great demand due to his good knowledge of the Hindu customs and traditions. Also, he was a respected palmist. People called him over to their homes for the religious functions because he charged less than other priests in the town. Despite doing such sundry jobs his earnings were barely enough to support his large family.

He lived in better times when things were cheap and one could live in comfort within limited resources. So, in his wisdom he didn't save anything for his five children, four of which were daughters. And the old man spent his entire earnings on his daughters' marriage and in the bargain there was little left for his son.

When Ramakant was in the final year of graduation his parents died within a span of few months, leaving him in a financial mess. They had left a dilapidated house of two rooms, a toilet, a kitchen and a veranda. It leaked during the rainy season and he had no money for the repairs. Luckily his father had left some money in the bank, bulk of which he used to clear the grocery bills, dues of the milkman and other debts. And the remaining amount saw him off for a few months until he got the tuition to sustain himself.

His father had taken no pains to teach him any good values. In fact, Ramakant didn't remember if his father ever hugged him and spoke a few words of comfort and encouragement. Like an orphan, he grew up in the midst of chaos, confusion and deprivation. Whatever qualities he had, were imbibed from watching people in the college, on the streets and elsewhere. So, he didn't weep when his father died. He didn't remember him afterwards, either, although he missed his mother sometimes. She loved her son and showed her affection in her own ways. His sisters were married into the rich families and lived a happy life. They seldom called him. He too wasn't fond of them. Moreover, he didn't visit them, lest they thought he wanted any monetary help from them. Too proud to ask money from anyone, he struggled to make his future.

For many years after his graduation he hunted for the paltry work to earn some money to sustain himself but the permanent job eluded him. He had seen the plight of several unemployed graduates who made daily rounds of one office or the other in search of employment.

While cleaning the home one day he found a rusted coin hidden behind the Lord Krishna's photo frame. Perplexed, he wondered why his father had kept that dirty bronze piece in such an obscure place. What bothered him further was that the old man had forgotten to tell him anything about it. It would be a worthless coin otherwise his father would have told him about it, he thought and replaced it.

Next day while visiting the *Assi Ghat* for a dip in the holy waters of the River Ganges, on the way he saw an Antique Shop. Curious, he sauntered into the store and asked the owner about the items displayed in the glass window. The shopkeeper told him that those items were the antiques and thus priceless. The price tags made his head spin. He couldn't imagine that those seemingly worthless items had such a huge value. Then it occurred to him that his coin too might be an antique and fetch him good money. He recalled his father reading the palms of the rich businessmen, anyone of them could have given him that coin as a reward.

Mustering up the courage, he said, "I've a similar looking coin, I mean an antique at home. Can I show it to you? I would like to sell it."

"Yeah. Get it tomorrow. I'll have a look," the busy shopkeeper said with a mechanical smile.

Later, Ramakant took a bath in the river and returned home. It was lunchtime but he wasn't hungry. He was eager to know the exact price of his coin but he didn't want to visit the shop that day and antagonize the owner. So, he started making lunch. After eating food he sat down to plan how to spend the money he thought he would get for the coin. Similar looking coins in the shop were priced at a couple of thousands. So, he guessed the coin could fetch him about two thousand rupees, which for a penniless person like him was a goldmine.

With that money he planned to buy a few pairs of shirts and trousers that he needed so badly. About a thousand rupees would be required for the groceries and the balance amount he would save for the rainy day. Thinking of the money he dozed off and woke up late in the evening. A long, cold night stood between the fortune and him. After dinner he made fresh expenditure plans and changed the plans made during the day. He was ecstatic about the money he visualized to get by selling the coin.

Dreaming about the money he went to bed. After a fitful sleep he woke up at dawn. The broken alarm clock had struck six a while ago. It was a misty winter morning. The day had not broken yet. Outside, it was still dark. He arose from the bed, made tea and then sat on the broken chair. The bedbugs bit him and spoiled the taste of tea and his mood.

In fact, every piece of furniture—beds, chairs, stools—was broken and needed urgent repairs but he had no money for that. He spent the cash on the essential groceries and other goods. Restless, he stared at the clock but the needles didn't seem to move. In needless anxiety he paced to and fro in the room. The clock struck nine. Quickly he dressed up and moved out to the Antique Shop with coin tucked inside his trouser pocket.

It was a chilly December morning. Most shops except the tea stalls were closed. A few shopkeepers, however, had sacrificed the comfort of the quilt and were opening the shutters. To his frustration the Antique Shop was shut. He sat at the nearby teashop and asked for tea, leafing through a Hindi daily. No news interested him. He glanced through the headlines to kill time.

Engrossed in thoughts he didn't notice that the Antique Shop had opened. The shopkeeper was busy in cleaning the shelves. He waited for him to finish before approaching him. Once he was sure the owner was free he walked to the shop and opened the glass door.

"Yes, what do you want?" the owner asked in a stern tone.

"Sorry. I haven't come to buy anything. You remember I spoke to you yesterday about an antique coin. I want to sell it," he spoke with a glint in his eyes.

"Let's see what have you got," the shopkeeper said hiding his irritation.

The man didn't entertain any sellers in the morning as he considered it inauspicious. Consumed with greed, he wanted to acquire the coin at a throwaway price from a simpleton and then sell it to some gullible foreigner at an exorbitant amount. That was his modus operandi. In fact, that way the most antique dealers worked in the holy city.

Ramakant fished out a dirty, rusted coin from his pocket, cleaned it with hankie and placed it on the glass counter as if it were a precious diamond. Then he looked at the owner with hope in his heart and sparkle in his eyes.

The curious shopkeeper lifted the coin, turned it upside down and rubbed it on his palm. Then he turned back, searched for the magnifying glass and looked through it. He wanted to be sure before taking a final decision. So, he had one last look at the coin before putting it down on the counter in disgust. Then he removed his specs and gave the seller a long stare.

Ramakant couldn't bear the long, killing silence any further and asked, "How much would I get for it?"

"Nothing," the shopkeeper shot back in suppressed anger.

"What!" he was shell-shocked.

"It's worthless. Keep it as a souvenir. For me it has no value," the shopkeeper spoke in a terse voice, signaling the end of their conversation and the end of Ramakant's dreams.

Crestfallen, he walked out of the shop. Ten minutes ago he had entered it with plenty of dreams and ten minutes later all those dreams lay shattered. He went to the river where he sat at the *ghat* and brooded over his future, which that moment looked bleaker than ever before.

And when he was about to fling the worthless coin in the water, someone shouted from behind. "Stop, don't do it. Who knows it might be priceless and change your destiny."

Surprised, he turned back and saw an ash-covered saint clothed in tatters standing on the steps of the *ghat*. He asked him, "*Baba*, why did you stop me?"

"*Beta*, let me see it."

He handed the coin to him. The saint had a close look at the coin and murmured, "*Beta*, this is a lucky coin, though it seems worthless in appearance. Whoever has this coin will get a fortune in the near future."

The saint handed back the coin to him and smiled.

"How soon will I get the fortune?" a puzzled Ramakant asked.

"In six months but don't ask me how. Only Lord Ram knows because He is the one who bestows the mortals with everything."

"*Baba*, why do you play cruel joke on me?" he whispered.

"No, *beta*. This isn't a joke. It's the truth. I can bet my life on it. My predictions have never gone wrong," the saint raised his voice.

"All right, *baba*, I believe you but I've nothing to give in return for your prophecy," he was apologetic.

"A cup of tea would do," the saint smiled and added as an afterthought, "But remember one thing; the fortune will stay with you as long as this lucky coin is in your possession. So, don't ever lose it at any cost."

After drinking tea the saint walked away singing a *bhajan*. Ramakant remained in a state of trance for sometime and kept looking at the coin. Later he returned home and tried to forget the saint's prophecy about the coin that morning as a joke. Then he spent the next five months in utter poverty.

One fine summer morning when he read in the local Hindi daily that a beggar had won ten-lakh rupees in the lottery. It struck him where his hidden fortune lay. So he went to the lottery vendor and bought a ticket for ten rupees. The first prize offered was ten lakhs.

At home he kept the ticket at the Lord Krishna's photo and prayed each day. The draw was a week away but the time moved at a snail's pace. And when the wait got over, he went to the vendor and asked him about the result. As the numbers were tallied, his heartbeat increased. When the vendor broke the news to him that he had won the first prize, he almost fainted in excitement and disbelief.

Since that day his entire life changed for the worse. The money made him greedier and insecure. When he had nothing, he slept well without bothering about the theft. The thieves knew he was a pauper. At times when he forgot to shut the main door he found nothing missing from the house the next morning. He then realized he was safe from any burglary.

But after receiving the fortune, he knew things would change. Sooner or later, the gangsters in the city would learn of his vast wealth and come knocking at his doors. He felt a chill run down his spine and the beads of sweat fill his forehead. He was sure his life would be threatened once he collected the prize and at any cost he didn't want to part with his hard-earned money; that's what he thought of his lottery prize.

Besides thieves, there were others too. His friends, cousins, sisters and brothers-in-law who so far had no time to look him up but once they heard about his money would flock to him like vultures. So, he continued to stay in the same old house and didn't carry out any repairs. A few of his well-wishers advised him to put the money in the bank, but he refused. Instead, he converted his prize into thousand rupee notes and buried it under the kitchen. He was afraid that if he flaunted his wealth the relatives, friends and goons would swindle it. Often the saint's words echoed in his mind and so, he guarded the lucky coin zealously.

Then one day he sold off his parental house, left Varanasi and went to Jabalpur. He purchased a modest house there and lived incognito. After a few months he realized it was getting difficult to hide such a large amount of money without inviting suspicion from the neighbours. After a month when a neighbour told him that some men from Varanasi were looking for him, he got alerted. It occurred to him that they might be the gangsters. So, that night he struck a deal with his neighbour, sold off his house at a loss and escaped in the wee hours.

Next morning when the goons came they found his house locked. They went on a wild goose chase in his search. Ramakant took a bus for Nagpur in Maharashtra where he stayed for a few months and then left that place and went into the hiding in Hyderabad. And there also he couldn't stay for long when his pursuers came after him. He had to escape from there too. By then he began to curse the day he had got the money. But he had no other choice than to protect it.

From Hyderabad he took a train to Bhopal and then boarded a bus for Bilaspur. The bus was full except for the last row. He occupied the corner window seat, placed his suitcase underneath, secured it with a lock and chain, and sighed with relief. His co-passenger, who had kept an eye on his actions, said, "It seems you are carrying something valuable in it."

He fumbled, fidgeted on the seat, regained his composure and replied, "No, no, there's nothing valuable. It has a few old clothes and some papers."

Then he opened a book and pretended to read it. Out of the corner of his eye he saw the co-passenger and found him staring at his suitcase. The wily man wasn't convinced and so, he would have to be vigilant about the suitcase during the journey. On a previous occasion he had almost lost the coin when his attention had got diverted to the suitcase. But somehow the coin had always come back to him. He knew that his fortune was linked to it and if he ever lost it he would become a pauper again.

"I'm Prakash," the man's gruff voice interrupted his thoughts. He turned right and saw an extended hand.

He said, giving a warm handshake, "I'm Ramakant," and fell silent. He hated talkative people but he knew there was no escape.

"Where are you going?" Prakash asked.

"Bilaspur."

"Me, too."

"I'm a teacher in the High School," Prakash said, looking at Ramakant in anticipation.

"I'm jobless and going to Bilaspur for an interview," Ramakant lied. Since the time he had got the lottery money, lies came naturally to him. Nowadays he rarely spoke the truth. He couldn't.

In spite of initial reservations, he liked Prakash and enjoyed talking with him. After sometime he shed his fear about his companion's suspect intentions. The duo continued their conversation on various subjects till they were about to reach Bilaspur. Ramakant alighted at the dhaba on the outskirts. He looked back at the bus and found Prakash getting down. He was stunned and got fearful but put on a normal face. He called him over, "Come, let's have tea."

"Yeah."

They watched the bus move towards the city. The sun had set. The dusk was spreading the blanket of chilled darkness. Ramakant had alighted there to avoid Prakash but he wondered why the latter had got down with him. Perhaps he had got the wind of the money hidden in the suitcase. Since the time he had boarded the bus at Bhopal, he had checked the coin once. His hand straightway went to the inner pocket of his shirt. It was empty. Fear gripped him. In shock, he started sweating. Then he stood up and searched the coin in every pocket, every bag. And when it was confirmed that he had lost it, he went hysterical.

"Oh, God! What'll I do now? I've lost my lucky coin, I'll lose the money too," he mumbled.

A puzzled, Prakash asked, "What happened?"

"You don't know. I've lost my lucky coin," he panted.

"What coin!"

"A rusted, old coin," he explained.

"It seems this coin is very important to you," Prakash gave a mischievous grin.

"Yeah, it is," Ramakant said, regaining his breath. "It's a lucky coin. Somebody gave it to my father. I found it hidden under the photo frame in my house. A saint told me that the holder of this coin will inherit a vast fortune."

"Yeah," Prakash said with a shrug. "You told me you've often lost it in the past but it has always come back to you."

"Yeah, always. So far it has never deserted me, but one can't be sure of one's destiny," Ramakant said in a pessimistic tone.

"How?"

"In the past people who found it were not greedy men and they returned it to me."

"Did everyone return the coin?"

"No. A few of them were greedy. I had to pay them a hefty price to get it back. And one man, in particular, gave me tough time but finally he..........."

"What!"

"He also saw the reason and returned the coin when he realized that it was of no use to him."

"So, you are willing to pay any price for it," Prakash said.

"Of course, any amount I've with me," Ramakant reiterated.

Prakash waited for a few seconds and then put his hand inside the jacket and took out a coin. He clutched it, extended the fist towards Ramakant and opened the fist, finger by finger, till the rusty coin showed up in his palm.

"Yeah, this is the coin, my lucky coin," an excited Ramakant yelled and bent forward to pick it up.

Prakash closed the fist and replaced the coin in the pocket. He heard the owner's vehement protests, "You can't keep it. It's mine. Give it to me."

"No, my friend. It was yours a while ago but now it belongs to me. It's mine," Prakash smiled.

"All right, I admit it's in your possession but please return it," Ramakant begged.

"OK, like others I'll also ask for its price. How much can you give me in cash, of course?" Prakash spoke like a businessman dealing with a pliant client.

"I can give you ten thousand rupees," Ramakant made his first offer keeping room for the negotiations later because he knew the greedy man sitting opposite him wouldn't agree for that paltry sum.

"Ten thousand," Prakash laughed out loud and called the waiter to bring more tea. "Ten thousand in exchange for a hidden fortune, I'm not that foolish, though I might look like one."

The waiter brought them hot tea and went back to attend to other customers. It had become dark. The dhaba owner switched on the lights. With every passing minute Ramakant got jittery.

A calm Prakash, sipping tea at leisure, said, "I'm sure the other people in the past wouldn't have settled for such a small amount."

That moment Ramakant felt he was dealing with a difficult man, perhaps a hardened criminal. Thought sent a chill down his spine and he perspired under the warm jacket he wore to protect himself from the cold. Regaining his poise, he renewed the offer, "All right, I can give you twenty thousand rupees."

As expected Prakash's reaction was nonchalant and peeved. He urged Ramakant to increase his bid and they bargained for some time. The last offer was for one lakh, which Prakash refused and then he made a bizarre demand when he saw their bargain making no headway, "All right, don't give me any money. Give me your old suitcase."

"Suitcase!" Ramakant almost jumped in fright.

"Yeah, suitcase. You told me it has nothing except a few old clothes. I'll settle for it," Prakash gave a mysterious grin.

So, Prakash knew what was there in the suitcase. The man was smarter than Ramakant had imagined. He cleared his throat and said, "What if I refuse to give you the suitcase?"

"It's simple. Then you don't get the coin," Prakash said. "It'll bring me the fortune."

"I can snatch it from you," Ramakant spoke in an intimidating tone.

"You can't. I'll swallow the coin," Prakash shrugged.

"All right, I guess I've no other choice but to give you the suitcase," he handed the suitcase to Prakash who mocked, returning him the coin, "People who returned you the coin were fools. Perhaps they didn't know that you carried your fortune in this bag."

"But I told you whoever has the lucky coin keeps the fortune," Ramakant argued.

"I would be a fool to believe your gibberish. The truth is that I have your fortune and you are a pauper. It will take some time to sink in your head," Prakash laughed. "Have your coin; you can acquire the fortune later."

Ramakant held the coin in his fist and put it in his pant pocket. Then he saw Prakash walk away with his fortune. He stood up and followed him. It was dark and he couldn't see Prakash but heard his footsteps.

He shouted, "Prakash, you haven't heard the last thing about the coin." Prakash halted and he closed on him.

"You said something about that useless coin," Prakash mocked.

"Yeah. I forgot to tell you this coin brings misfortune to anyone, other than me, who touches it."

"You can't be serious," Prakash laughed. "Come on, go home and don't bore me further. I had enough of your nonsense already. Now it's time for me to enjoy the wealth I'm carrying."

"Prakash, neither you are the first man, nor you would be the last one to walk away with my fortune. In the past a few men tried but didn't succeed. I forgot to tell you that I had to kill them to get my money back," Ramakant had assumed the countenance a killer.

Unfazed, Prakash resumed walking. Then he heard the shots being fired from behind and bullets pierce his body, his heart. He fell on the ground and died instantly. Ramakant went closer to him, picked up the suitcase and said, “I wish you had paid heed to my warning and believed me.”

He walked away murmuring, “Didn’t I tell you whoever has the coin keeps the fortune? You did the mistake of selling it.”

Repentance

On a pleasant October evening the platform number four of the New Delhi Railway Station was jam-packed with passengers, their friends and relatives who had come to see them off. They all waited for The Ranikhet Exp to move out. The train whistled a couple of times. The green signal was on but the guard, in the faded dress, chatted with his friends. He showed no urgency. Some passengers had occupied their seats and the rest who knew how the railway functioned, waited on the platform in needless anxiety. A few travellers shopped for the books, magazines, snacks, tea and bottled water. The latecomers with coolies in tow rushed towards the train and searched for their seats.

Finally, the driver's patience ran out and the train moved with a long shrill whistle. In the midst of bedlam the passengers on the platform rushed in, pushing people in the gallery and inviting their angry stares.

"Thank God! The train's late otherwise I would have missed it today also. Delhi has become overpopulated with traffic jams everywhere," a woman in mid-thirties mumbled and then yelled at the coolie, "*Bhaiya*, berth 32 is here. Get the luggage fast. The train has started moving."

"I've reservation for A 32," she said to another woman sitting on that seat.

"Yeah, it's yours. Mine is the upper one," the second woman said, and shifted to the opposite berth making room for her.

"Take this," she said handing a fifty-rupee note to the coolie."

"Thank you, memsahib," the coolie pocketed the money and jumped out.

Within a few minutes, the train picked up speed and left the city lights behind. It was 9 p.m. Lateness of the train by fifteen minutes had enabled her to board it in time. Through the tinted, unclean windows of the air-conditioned coupe, both the women, with mixed feelings, watched the darkness swallow the city. They were escaping from Delhi for different reasons. One was returning home to join her husband in Nainital, while the other to stay with her mother in Ranikhet after a fight with her husband. After a while they looked at each other, exchanged smiles and got into conversation.

"I'm Divya," said the first woman extending her hand and found the hand of her co-passenger warm, soft and a bit sweaty.

"I'm Shivani. Shivani Rawat. That's my maiden name which I insisted to keep after marriage despite my husband's strong misgivings," spoke the second woman, who had boarded the moving train.

Both fell silent for a moment.

"I'm going to Nainital to join my husband. I had come to Delhi to look up my ailing aunt," said Shivani and then put her hand in the handbag and fished out a hand mirror, hair clip and lipstick. She pulled her hair back and put on the clip. Then she retouched her lips, a lighter shade of brown, and replaced the items in the bag. A quick stolen glance at the co-passenger gave her delight and relief. But Divya's gaze forced her to hide her triumphant grin.

Later, she pulled her legs up on the seat and made herself comfortable. They were the only passengers in that coupe, meant for four, and it gave them the confidence as the other two seats were not booked. After a while, in walked the travelling ticket examiner wearing crumpled white trousers, black coat faded at the elbows and collar, and a black tie. He matched their tickets with the chart, glanced at their IDs and asked them to be alert as a few women were travelling in that compartment. They fumed in indignation on his casual remark on such an important issue of women safety.

"Where do you live in Nainital?" asked Divya.

"My house is a furlong from Naina Devi Temple. My hubby is an author. He is writing about the tribes of Kumaon. The book keeps him busy," Shivani spoke with a tinge of sadness in her eyes.

"Do you have kids?"

"Yeah, a son. He is in the boarding school."

Then they shared a brief silence.

"Don't you think the writers are different from others? I mean no pun intended for your husband," Divya broke the silence.

"Yeah, you couldn't be more right. They are dreamers and often lost in thoughts. At times it becomes quite unsettling," Shivani said with a faint smile. She gazed into Divya's eyes and asked, "Your hubby?"

"He is an exporter in Delhi. Ours is a garment business," Divya said, with a forced smile.

"That's great. I mean being married to a millionaire. One doesn't have to worry about the money like middle class housewives. I heard the rich men are fun-loving too," her eyes sparkled as she spoke.

"Hmm, in a way yes if that's what you mean, but at some point in life the money fails to inspire you. It remains a necessity like eating and drinking. As far as my hubby is concerned, he's more fun-loving than I can handle," Divya hid her anguish behind her smile.

"I beg to differ. Money is important to those who don't have enough of it," Shivani said.

"Maybe. But for those people who have too much of it, it ceases to have any significance."

"That's the irony of life. Isn't it?"

"Yeah."

Their talks ended abruptly. They unpacked dinner, consisting of paranthas, vegetables and pickles, and shared the food. They craved for hot tea but at that late hour it was difficult to get as the next station was far away and the train had no pantry car. So, they had to curb their urge.

Putting the leftover in the plastic bag they stood up and threw it in the dustbin. While Shivani returned to coupe, Divya went to the toilet. Since neither of them felt sleepy, they resumed their conversation.

Divya, the more talkative of the two, took the lead and asked Shivani, "Tell me, how is life with a writer? I mean how exciting it is."

"It's OK, sometimes thrilling but often boring. I guess it would be with any man. Marriage is a complex and intricate relationship. Every couple goes through with its highs and lows," Shivani was nonchalant.

"I meant it's so romantic for a woman to have someone write poetry for her, give her a poem and not flowers on her birthday. It's so different, so out of the world," Divya said.

"Yeah, once in a while, it's a nice feeling but women like to be pampered with the clothes and jewellery," Shivani winked.

"Yes, but the ornaments have no real meaning in life. To me the honest relationship is more important," said Divya.

"What do you mean?"

"Being honest to each other and not cheating your spouse by sleeping around with others," Divya clarified.

"Is it an issue in today's world? Adultery had become commonplace even in the small towns and cities. How can one keep a check when both spouses travel often for work and deal with the opposite sex every day? It's human to succumb to the temptation," Shivani expressed her reservations.

"Whatever you might feel and say, honesty in the relation between spouses will remain an important issue as long as the civil society exists," insisted Divya.

"Maybe what you say has a meaning, but to me it seems funny that people should view faithfulness as the sole virtue upon which the relationship should hinge," Shivani argued without much conviction.

For a moment they stopped as the train passed through the station. The engine let off a loud whistle. Both peeped out in the dark and tried to get the name of the station. The night often did strange things to different people. It aroused awe in some, melancholy in some and romance in others. But they, Divya and Shivani, sought something different from the above.

Divya stood up, opened the bag and pulled out a steel thermos flask. She asked Shivani uncorking it, "Would you care for some coffee?

"Arey, why didn't you give it with dinner?"

"Oh, it slipped out of mind then. I recollected when I saw the station."

"Thanks. Coffee is my weakness. I can drink it anytime of the day or night. In fact, if one wakes me up in the middle of the night and offers it, I won't refuse," Shivani's face lit up.

"I hope it's hot. The company advertises that their flasks keep drinks hot or cold up to twenty-four hours. Let's check their claim," Divya said pouring coffee in two glasses.

"Wow! It's hot. Thanks," Shivani was ecstatic.

They sipped coffee at leisure, exchanging smiles in between. Shivani had a great passion for coffee and she often had it with her husband in the lawn and in the balcony, watching the sun set behind the distant hills. Those moments were precious for her, as he often discussed with her the theme, characters and plot of his novel. She listened to him in rapt attention and gave her suggestions, which he never forgot to include. He valued her ideas and admired her intelligence.

"Where have you got lost? Thinking about hubby," Divya interrupted her thoughts.

"Yeah, you're right. Coffee reminds me of him. He discusses his book with me over a cup of coffee," she sighed.

"Lucky girl. At least your man has time to drink coffee with you. My hubby doesn't have time to sit with me even for a few minutes. I often eat alone. I can't recall when we last had dinner together. For him money and business come first. I get the last priority," Divya complained.

"You are being harsh to him. Though I've no businessmen in the family, I empathize with them. After all, running business requires a lot of time and hard work," Shivani remarked.

"You're right but earning money isn't everything in life. He ought to give time to me too. I don't know how to spend time alone in a large bungalow," Divya complained.

"Maybe you should join the kitty parties or spend time in social activities about which we read in the newspapers and magazines," Shivani said.

"I wish I could but I'm not like them. I grew up in a small place and my mindset is different. I'm averse to the parties and social work. I find these things a big sham."

"But to me the media and the peer attention that come with social work are quite exciting."

"But I find it boring; in fact, vulgar and farcical."

Their discussion was getting serious, so Shivani changed the topic, "What about your kids? I mean where they are?"

"I've none. We haven't decided yet. Perhaps we will plan in a year or so," Divya's voice deepened with sadness. Though she wanted child, her husband had shown no interest so far. He had avoided the issue for the reasons best known to him.

"Oh, it's good to have kids because when husband goes away they give mother a good company."

"Yeah, but I can't produce them alone. I need his help," Divya gave a mischievous grin, bringing smile on Shivani's face.

"Isn't it strange and funny that it's the woman who carries the child in her womb, still she has no say in the matter when and how many children she should give birth to? It's always the man who has the last say."

"Yeah, it's a man's world whether we like it or not. So, next time when God asks for your choice, request Him to make you a man," Shivani teased.

"No, I didn't mean that. I'm better off as a woman," Shivani shot back.

Loud rattle of the bogey wheels and the shrill engine whistles interrupted their talks. Disruption had become a routine. When the train crossed the station or the bridge, it made loud noises in whose din it was impossible for the women to hear each other.

"What's the time?" Shivani asked.

"11 p.m.," said Divya, "I hope I'm not keeping you awake. If you want you can go to sleep. I'll take some more time."

"No. I'm not sleepy," said Shivani.

"Where do you plan to spend your holidays?" Shivani asked.

"With my mother in Ranikhet. She is alone at home. It would be great to spend some time with her."

"And where's your father?"

"He lives alone in Mumbai. He left my mother a decade ago."

"Oh, I'm so sorry."

"It's all right. I've forgotten him long back."

"If you don't mind may I ask what led to their break-up?"

"I'm not sure. I was twelve years old when I came to know of his decision. I was in the hostel then. Mother came and told me that father and she had filed for divorce and soon they would be separated. Since father wasn't keen to take me with him, the onus of raising me up fell upon my mother."

"It's tragic."

"I don't think so when I read about the thousands of girls who carry on with their struggles without any parental help. At least I've my mother to take care of me."

"That's the spirit. I like your philosophy of life," Shivani tried to cheer her companion up.

"What philosophy, yaar. I keep up a positive attitude," Divya smiled.

Shivani felt relieved when Divya regained her pleasing demeanour. She was thankful to God for giving her a great childhood with loving parents, though she was the third child after two sons.

"I understand how hard it would have been for you till now," Shivani empathized.

"It's sweet of you," Divya said.

"We get one life and we should enjoy it well. I'll pray your hubby spends quality time with you in future," Shivani spoke with an endearing smile.

"How can I complain? I'm to blame for my present condition," Divya's past shadowed the glow on her face.

"Why? You shouldn't say that."

"Perhaps you don't know. I had someone who loved me and cared for me until I dumped him because of my stupidity."

"You mean this is your second marriage."

"Yeah."

Shivani waited with abated breath to hear the story. Divya looked out in the cold darkness of the night and began, "It was six years ago. After my post graduation I worked in the Imperial Hotel in Nainital as a receptionist. The job was to tide over the financial crisis my mother faced. She had no bank balance or property, except for a modest house in Ranikhet. Though some people advised her to ask maintenance from my father and if he refused then file a case against him, my mother refused to approach him. She was too proud to ask him for alimony. My mother would have preferred to die than beg money from the man who had dumped her for a younger woman. I respected her decision then. In fact, I respect it more now.

Neither did I meet my father, nor asked him for any monetary help. I didn't want to see his face. It's a different matter that he never bothered to contact any of us either. Our lives were better without him. Mother shifted to Nainital where we rented a house. After about a year I met a man who had come to the hotel for the seminar on the wild life in the Himalayas organized under the aegis of the World Wildlife Fund (WWF). Later, I gathered that he was an important speaker during the seminar because of the extensive research he had done on the subject.

Ours was a chance meeting. One day when I was at the reception I saw a bearded man wearing the kurta pajama walk up to the counter and ask me about a foreign delegate. My first reaction to his bucolic appearance was of amusement and surprise. I wondered what that rustic man was doing in a three star hotel. I tried hard to suppress my smile but couldn't escape his sharp eyes. Perhaps he was in a hurry and so he didn't say anything then but in the evening when I returned to resume my duty I found a note lying for me. It read:

Dear Divya,

The world is not what our eyes see but, in fact, the truth always remains hidden till such time it's explored. And a few people have the time and courage to explore the truth while the silent majority lives a life based on false notions and convictions.

Yours,

Rustic

That note stung me like a bee and for the next few days I stayed dazed and felt ashamed. The man had read my eyes and interpreted my smile. I got attracted to him and so, I obtained his whereabouts. After a while we began dating and a few months later we got married. He was a writer but I considered him an explorer. Before writing on any subject he would go to any length to explore the facts and details, and then undertake the writing. I hope he doesn't resemble your hubby?" Divya looked at Shivani in the dim light of the compartment and asked.

"No, no. He is not a fastidious man as you've described. In fact, he is too lazy to work on the details. He is a writer but the similarities end there," Shivani said nonchalantly.

"What is he passionate about in writing?" Divya asked to clarify a few of her concerns.

"He writes fiction for which he doesn't do much research. By the way, you were telling me about your first hubby," Shivani reminded her.

"Yeah, I told you how we met and dated. He was a compassionate man who had a soft corner for the poor. When we walked together he would stop and ask people on the street how they earned their livelihood. Often he would give them money and move ahead. What surprised me the most was that he needed money to build the house but that didn't deter him from helping out the poor and needy.

And one day the lady luck smiled on him and he received a huge royalty for the book. With that money he purchased an old bungalow on the hillock in Nainital, wherein he shifted with his meager belongings, consisting of a box full of old clothes, an old typewriter and some books. I helped him in setting up the new house and then to my utter surprise and delight he proposed me. I accepted and the following month we got married in a simple ceremony.

My life was blissful for about a year. Living with a wonderful man in the beautiful hill station was a dream. During the weekends we went for trekking in the mountains and spent nights in the forlorn gaddi huts. It was a prolonged honeymoon that lasted about a year," Divya paused to take a breather.

The word, 'honeymoon' made Shivani blush. Unable to control herself, she asked, "If you don't mind, may I ask you something personal?"

"Hmm," Divya nodded.

"How was it with him? I mean..." Shivani couldn't hide her awkwardness.

"You mean physically," Divya waited for a moment and then spoke with a grin, "Yeah, he was good, nothing out of the world but passionate and frequent. I had never visualized my life without him. We lived a contented life but were often short of money, about which he never complained but I felt the pinch. I wanted to acquire better things for us but he wasn't interested. For him the life revolved around his books. And when he worked on the manuscript he forgot everything—eating, drinking, shaving, bathing or talking. When I whined, he would urge me to go for a walk around the lake and leave him alone.

And during an evening walk around the Naini Lake I met a handsome guy. Perhaps he had approached me finding a melancholic woman sitting by herself. He was dashing and confident. At the first instance he introduced himself and asked me for coffee. Though I was hesitant to go with a stranger, his courteous behavior bowled me over. While sipping coffee I stole many glances at him and found his persona exude a strange magnetism, which was difficult for me to ward off. Thereafter, we met several times as he was holidaying alone. Those days were trying times for me, both mentally and physically, as my husband was busy and gave me little time. His neglect willy-nilly pushed me into the waiting arms of another man. And we overstepped the boundary of our friendship on the last night of his stay. He promised to marry me after I divorced my husband. The man gave me dreams, real big dreams of life in a metro. He owned a huge house with a battery of servants and earned loads of money.

The lure of lucre and his physical prowess were too tempting for me to leave and hence I planned to dump my husband, a penniless writer, who had little time for my emotional or physical needs. So, I started working towards achieving my goal and in a couple of months my persistent nagging and howling threw our lives asunder. To my delight one day he suggested that if I wasn't happy with him it was better for both of us to separate and end the bitterness that was destroying our lives. With a smile he signed the divorce papers and we separated on an amicable note. Next day I resigned from my job and moved to Delhi. We were married in the palatial house of my new husband.

I couldn't believe my luck of marrying a prince and living with him a fairytale life about which the girls read in the story books. We went for our honeymoon to Switzerland and after that I accompanied him on many foreign trips. And then one day my world, which I had built with fidelity, honesty and hard work fell apart when I found out that my husband was sleeping around with not one but many girls. The man is a womanizer.

Now I realize how important it is to have a man devoted to you and you alone in mind and body. Despite all his shortcomings my first husband was an honest man and valued loyalty high in marriage. Having burnt my fingers I repent now that I left him at the spur of the moment, hankering for a wealthy lifestyle. What my first husband gave me perhaps I would never get in my life ever. I still remember he would come running to me and share his first thought of his new book. I would listen to him and give my stupid suggestions, which he often found useful. He respected me more for my intelligence than body. On the contrary, my present husband treats me like a good body, which satisfies his carnal desires when at home because while he is away he buys sex.

Divya paused to wipe her moist eyes. The story had moved Shivani who waited for Divya to regain her calm before clarifying a doubt, "If you are in a bad marriage, why don't you leave him?"

"It's not that easy. How long can I hunt for Mr. Right and then what's the guarantee the next man would be a good human being? More so, I'm tired and have no heart for experimenting all my life. Continuing in the present relationship in a way is my atonement for hurting a good man. Good or bad, for me the life would go on like this," Divya sank in the sea of sadness.

"Suppose your first husband were to forgive you and call you back in his life tomorrow, what will be your response?" Shivani's abrupt and strange question pulled Divya out of her melancholy.

"God can't be so generous again after watching me botch it up the first time," she was despondent.

"Forget it. Sorry, I bothered you with my story. Tell me something about your hubby. Are you missing him?" Divya forced a smile on her face.

"When I think of him I wonder how he can be so lazy. You know when I'm not at home he would make a mess of the house and live in it without any hassles. Used plates and cups would lie all around the house. More clothes would be out of the cupboard than inside it. The sheets and pillows would be lying everywhere; in the drawing-room, bedroom and study. To my surprise, he doesn't behave that way when I'm around. In fact, it's cute of him that he makes sure to clear the mess created by him before I enter the house. I can visualize what he would be doing at this moment. He would be cleaning the rooms, and replacing the clothes and books in the cupboards and shelves. Prior to my arrival he would tidy up the house. He would be changing the sheets, pillow covers, dusting the house and refilling the empty water bottles. He would keep awake tonight in my wait and greet me with red eyes when I meet him tomorrow. Though clumsy, he is cute and takes care of me in a true sense. With him I find happiness in small things of life. I love my man and would never leave him," Shivani spoke but felt foolish for saying the last sentence, which could hurt Divya.

"How stupid of me? You are telling me about the man whose name I don't know," Divya said.

"Abhi..."

"Abhinav," Divya prompted.

"No. Abhishek," said Shivani. Both women sighed with relief.

"Nice to know you are happy in marriage. I wish you both long years of togetherness," Divya said and made a conscious effort to search for her watch in the handbag. Then she said with surprise, "Oh my God! It's past midnight. We should catch some sleep otherwise your hubby will blame me for keeping his sweetheart awake throughout the night."

She looked at Shivani and winked. When Divya went out of the coupe for a while, Shivani took out a piece of paper and scribbled a note, and then pushed it in the inner pocket of Divya's handbag before her return.

"Aren't you going to the washroom?" Divya asked.

"Yeah."

After sometime they switched off the night lamp and slept. Next morning they woke up when the train stopped at Kathgodam. They alighted and looked for the coolie.

"Thanks for the nice company. Keep in touch," Divya hugged Shivani.

"Sure, give my love to auntie. And if possible drop in at my place when you come to Nainital," Shivani said handing her visiting card.

Divya placed it in her bag. They exchanged affectionate smiles and parted.

In the evening at Ranikhet, Divya while searching for something emptied her handbag on the bed and was surprised to find a paper. She opened it and read:

Dear Divya,

You would be shocked to know that the man you had left some years ago is with me. I mean I'm married to him now, though he has changed a lot in the past years. After you moved away from him he has lost much of his originality. You've lost a good husband and the world a good writer. What I've is a simple, good human being. Be assured, I will take good care of him as you would wish to.

Shivani.

Divya read the note again and again, tears rolling down her eyes. Later she prayed for both, Abhinav and Shivani.

Those Seven Days

Since last two days Anant Hegde had been lying in the bed with a mild fever. He had taken a paracetamol but the fever hadn't subsided. His friends had visited him and a few of them had urged him to see the doctor. He didn't feel like eating anything but drank plenty of fruit juices. His thoughts wavered around his absence from the job and pending work lying at his desk. And then the doorbell rang. Its shrill sound irritated him. Grudgingly he stood up to open the door. His face lit up seeing Shikha at the doorstep.

"What a pleasant surprise. I would have killed the person if it weren't you, Shikha," he smiled.

"Thank God. I saved you from going to the gallows," she winked and walked in closing the door.

Both went to the bedroom and before she could sit down, he asked, "Shikha, can you make me tea, please?"

"Sure," she said and went to the kitchen. After putting the tea on the gas to boil she returned and asked, "Did you take your temperature in the morning?"

"No."

"Open your mouth. Not that big, you stupid. I'm going to take your temperature," she scolded.

He blushed and relaxed his jaws. She put the thermometer in his mouth and instructed, "Hold it till I return."

The kitchen air was filled with the aroma of the Darjeeling tea. She poured it into two mugs, picked up some biscuits and returned to him. Putting cups on the bedside table, she pulled the thermometer out and strained her eyes to read it against the tube light. The mercury touched 104 degree Fahrenheit.

"Oh my God! It's quite high. Let me see your forehead," she placed her tender palm on his forehead and almost jumped in fright, "Anant, you're burning. Did you see the doctor today?"

"Forget it. Let's have tea," he said.

"Don't take it lightly. Have tea fast and get ready. I'm taking you to the nursing home just now" she insisted.

They had tea together, she in hurry and he at leisure, and then he changed his clothes and she drove him to the Leela Nursing Home, owned by Dr Krishna Patil. At the reception they filled the mandatory forms and then a nurse took them to the medical specialist.

"Don't worry; he'll be OK within a few days. It's a viral infection but since he has a high fever we will keep him under observation for a few days," Dr Shoumya Chatterjee tried to encourage Shikha, who looked perturbed.

After completing the formalities, Anant was admitted and taken to an air-conditioned room. A few moments later a nurse came and took some blood samples and went away. Shikha stayed with him for a couple of hours and then returned to his apartment to fetch his clothes, toiletries, books, etc. En route, she told their common friends who rushed to the hospital hearing about his illness.

"Arey yaar, what happened? You were OK when I met you the other day," Manish asked entering the room.

"Nothing serious. It's just a fever. Shikha showed me to the doctor, who has kept me under observation for a few days since my temperature is high," Anant explained.

"Don't worry, you will get well soon," comforted Shailesh.

"I will tell the boss in the office tomorrow about it and request him to grant you leave," Rajiv said.

"Does his boss have any other option?" Ritesh quipped.

"All bosses are heartless. They don't see anything except their company's interest," spoke Reena with bitterness.

"No, they aren't as heartless as you think. Have you ever tried to peep into your boss's lonely heart?" Avinash teased.

"Shut up," she yelled back.

In the meanwhile a nurse, with a stethoscope around her neck, walked in. She was a tall, beautiful girl with pleasing demeanour. Like other nurses, she worked as a trainee in the nursing home. When she entered the room they stopped talking and for a moment their eyes stayed at her face.

She smiled and said, "Will you all please step aside? I've to take his temperature," and then she put the thermometer in Anant's mouth.

When she was counting the pulse, she heard heavy sighs of the boys behind her. But unmindful, she readied to take the patient's BP. She asked him to roll over his shirtsleeve and then wrapped the rubber around his arm, and began measuring his BP. As she placed her fingers on his wrist she felt his body burning. Once finished, she closed the instrument.

"Sister, I hope my BP is normal," Anant looked worried.

"Yeah, nothing to worry about. You'll get well soon," she patted him and turned to leave. All male gazes followed her. And when she was out of the room, Anant's friends let off loud sighs and moans.

"Hey guys, stop ogling. She is gone," Anant taunted.

"Boss, you'll recover soon with such pretty nurses to take care of you," Avinash said rolling his eyes.

Munish leaned and spoke in a conspiratorial whisper to Anant, “I heard nurses take real good care of their patients.”

Shikha, who had walked in unannounced, kept his clothes, toiletries and books in the side cupboard. She didn’t disturb Anant as she saw him in animated conversation with Munish. Both smiled in between. She felt relieved.

Despite high fever, Anant couldn’t control his glee. By their looks she knew Munish was up to some mischief. The friends stayed with him for another hour and regaled him with their stale jokes, anecdotes and stories. As long as they stayed Anant forgot his pain and believed he would soon be out of the nursing room and be with them. As the evening approached and the visitors’ time limit was to expire, he began to feel lonely. At 5 p.m. they all left promising to look him up the next day. They all shook hands and wished him a speedy recovery.

Shikha was the last person to leave. Before moving out she tied up with the hospital authorities about his food and medicines.

“Anant, I’ll go now. I’ve spoken to the nurse, who will watch your temperature. In case of an emergency, press the bell,” she hugged him and kissed. Separating, she spoke with misty eyes, “Don’t worry, you’ll get well soon. I will pray for your speedy recovery.”

He saw her off till the gate and watched her leave the premises. Later he returned to his room and read the magazines brought by her. He read them all one by one, some before and remaining after dinner. Killing time was a big problem with no TV or music system. He thought about his fiancée, whom he was to wed in September after three months. She was a sensitive, caring and understanding girl. Both worked in the same company and theirs was love at first sight. They had dated for almost a year now. A month ago both had met each other’s parents and sought their consent.

In fact, Anant's parents were glad to meet her and wanted an early marriage.

Shikha had charmed her way into her prospective in-law's hearts with her simplicity, beauty and values. Anant was excited about the marriage and counted days on the calendar. She had been a positive influence in his life since the day he had met her. When alone, he felt incomplete. Her presence brought a fresh breeze and filled his life with fragrance.

When the duty nurse came and asked him to switch off the lights and go to sleep, he looked at her and remembered what Munish had said in the evening. A smile ran on his face. The nurse smiled back and left. Later he fell asleep.

On the first day the doctors gave him treatment for viral fever and from the next day when his blood report came, they treated him for malaria. The anti-malarial tablets and capsules were bitter and he swallowed them, and then ate chocolate to get over the bitter taste.

As promised his friends visited him the next afternoon. Shikha was the first to arrive and the last to leave. And every day more friends came to see him. It was his fifth day in the nursing home and the fever hadn't come down. He got worried and asked the doctor, "Doc, when I will get well?"

"Don't worry, you will be OK within a few days," the doctor said with a forced smile and then told his friends, "You guys, pep him up."

A worried doctor returned to the cabin and thought of consulting his senior, Dr Lokesh Kesarvani. He entered the latter's office, sat down on the sofa and waited for him to finish with his secretary. Once he was free, Dr Kesarvani turned towards him and asked, "Yes, Doctor Chatterjee, I hope everything is all right."

"No, Sir. One of my patients, Anant, is having a high fever. I've treated him for viral and malaria but the fever is not coming down. I suggest we send his blood sample for the HIV test," Dr Chatterjee looked worried.

"All right, but don't tell either the patient or any of his acquaintances. Minimum people in the hospital should know about it," Dr Kesarvani advised, "In the meantime continue his treatment for viral, if he hasn't tested positive for malaria."

After a few minutes the doctor returned to his cabin. For next couple of days his friends including Shikha visited him daily and cheered him up. More than the nurses, Shikha took care of his every need. She sat by his bed for long hours and put wet towel over his head to bring down the temperature. Often his friends joked with him about her and teased that she was behaving like a wife. He smiled and then wandered off in her thoughts. He was desperate to get well soon so that he could resume work, and plan his future life with her. In the hospital the staff or friends always surrounded him and he didn't get any time with her in privacy.

"Anant, have you told your mummy, papa about your illness?" she asked him putting the flask on the table.

"No, I don't want to bother them. I'll speak to them once I get out of this hole," he sounded dejected.

"Don't worry, you'll get well soon," she patted him.

As had been her routine for the last five days, she stayed with him till evening and then left wishing him goodnight. Later he read the magazines once she left and kept awake till 11 p.m. He slept when the duty nurse scolded him. "It's not good for you to keep late nights. Good sleep will help you to recover faster," she said switching off the light.

Day One

And the hell broke loose when his blood report arrived. He had tested positive for the HIV. His report was kept a hush-hush affair in the hospital. Dr Chatterjee with Dr Kesarvani walked into his room and closed the door. All his friends had left by then. Their faces were grim and anxious. They pulled the chairs and sat at his bedside.

Dr Kesarvani cleared his throat and spoke, "Well Anant, I'm afraid we have some real bad news for you. It's quite distressing."

"Tell me doctor, nothing is serious, I hope," Anant's face went pale.

"I'm afraid. It is. We had sent your blood sample to the laboratory for the HIV and you've tested positive," he dropped the bombshell and watched the patient go in a state of shock.

They knew he would get over it soon and waited for him to regain his poise. He was a brave man. After a while he put on a brave face and asked, "Doctor, how much time do I have?"

"As of now we are not sure because we need more tests but you should forget about it. Live life to the fullest. Remember, there is always light at the end of the tunnel. You are rich and can afford costly medicines. Good medication and emotional support from the loved ones can prolong life by several years. Maybe by then science might discover its cure," Dr Kesarvani tried to raise his morale.

"Anant, we would ask you a few things related to it. Hope you don't mind. We are asking this to find the reason. I know you are not married. Try to recollect whether you ever had unprotected sex with someone and if yes, then with whom," Dr Chatterjee asked.

For a moment he felt humiliated and belittled in front of his questioners. His character was under scrutiny but he knew they were doing their job. So he kept his feelings aside and said, "I don't recollect indulging in unprotected sex ever. In fact, you would be surprised that I seldom have sex."

"You can spend the night here. It would be better if you leave the hospital tomorrow and continue the treatment at home. We will call you for regular check-ups," they tried to make it as painless as possible for him.

So, he had become an unwanted patient in the hospital. It shocked him. He understood their dilemma and asked them to prepare his bills in the night so that he could leave in the morning. The doctors gave him a sympathetic glance and left. He looked at the white ceiling, painted in the colour of death. He had read the horror stories how the families, friends and relatives ill-treated the AIDS patients when they went home from the hospital. But he was sure that his fate would be better because his family, fiancée and friends were educated and caring. With their moral support he hoped to live a happy life. He wouldn't have to face the social ostracism unlike several other AIDS patients.

He was contemplating about his future when the duty nurse walked in and scolded, "I told you it's not good to keep awake. Go to sleep now."

The way she scolded him brought a smile of his face. She smiled back and left. She might not know about his disease otherwise she wouldn't have smiled, he thought. He had developed an affinity for her and was afraid to face her with his dreaded illness. Good, I would be gone tomorrow before she would see me again, he contemplated.

Anxieties, insecurities and uncertainties occupied his mind till late in the night and wore him down from within. Stillness of the night then took him into its lap and he slept.

Day Two

Next morning Dr Chatterjee was in the lobby when he saw Anant's friends enter the hospital. He called them aside and said, "Well, gentlemen I've some bad news for you. Your friend, Anant, has tested HIV positive. We are discharging him from the hospital today."

He then walked away. Anant's friends were shell-shocked unable to react. There was a pin-drop silence among them. They had never dreamed that their dear friend would meet such a fate. For a moment they were not sure how to react to that enormous tragic news. They had mixed feelings about his disease.

"We should meet him and give our moral support," said one friend.

"Have you gone mad? Don't you know the company of an AIDS patient is fraught with dangers," cautioned the second friend.

"I'm told one can acquire this disease by touching the infected person," said the third friend.

"No, we should keep away from him. He is going to die anyway. Why should we risk our lives?" advised the fourth friend.

Thereafter, a heated debate followed. The unreasonable voices smothered the sane voices. In minutes the empathetic friends swayed and went along with the decision of boycotting an AIDS victim. Barring a few friends, they left the hospital. While they were moving down the stairs, they saw Shikha approach them.

"Shikha, there is a terrible news. Doctor Chatterjee has told us that Anant has AIDS. You should keep away from him," one friend said, rushing out of the hospital.

Shikha was crestfallen and her first reaction was of shock and disbelief. She walked up to the doctor to crosscheck the news with him.

"Yeah, what you've heard is right. We are discharging him. If you want you can meet him. Though he hasn't told us, I think he has got it from an infected female," the doctor said and then got busy with other patients.

She returned to the corridor and found a few friends waiting. Along with them she went to Anant's room. As the door opened, a wry smile ran over his face and he greeted them. He extended his right hand, expecting a warm handshake from them but within seconds he withdrew it when he found their hands tucked in their trouser pockets. He firmed himself from within as he didn't want to show any signs of splitting up in front of them.

Most friends remained silent, though a couple of them spoke a few words of sympathy. Their voices lacked genuineness and made little impact on him. They stayed with him for less than a half-hour and assured him before leaving that he could count on them. His gaze followed them to the door. Thereafter, Shikha and he shared many glances. Both were too overwhelmed to say a word. He saw her dewy eyes filled with the questions of which he had no convincing answers. Neither that was the moment to give her any explanation, nor would she accept his innocence. It was one disease that in the first instance threw muck on the patient's character. After a few moments Shikha held his hand in hers and gave a quick, cold press. She said, "Anant, get well soon. I'll come and look you up."

Although he wanted to stop her and share his grief with her, he couldn't muster up the courage. With teary eyes, he watched her leave. Then he put his hand on the chest. He missed her tight hug, her hot breath, her sweet smell and her tender kisses. Those things always invigorated his heart and soul. Now she had walked away leaving him empty and helpless.

Outside the hospital, she burst out crying. Then she called up her father, "Papa, Anant has tested HIV positive."

"Shikha beta, please come here fast. We will discuss the matter and sort it out," he calmed her.

She headed for home. Her world fell into pieces before her eyes. She confided in her mother who was distressed to hear the bad news. Both waited for her father to come back from the office.

At the same time in the nursing home, the doctors told Anant to clear his bills and move out. Sudden change in the behaviour of the nurses and the ward boys gave him a feeling that they had come to know about his illness. So, he had become an outcast who could threaten their lives if they touched him even by mistake.

All of a sudden he was confronted with this harsh, naked reality. He paid up the bills, hired a taxi and reached his apartment. During the journey he tried to call Shikha but her cell phone was off. At home he rang her again but got no answer. He wondered why most of his friends had stayed away from him in the hospital that day. He had hoped her to stay with him for some time but she too had left without saying anything. Somehow his heart wasn't ready to accept the sudden change in her behaviour.

Later he abandoned his efforts to call anyone in the city and instead thought of telling his father, a retired government servant, living in Shimoga.

"Papa, I'm Anant speaking," he said and began crying.

"Anant beta, what happened, why are you crying? I hope everything is all right," his father at the other end got worried.

"Papa, I've got AIDS," his voice choked.

"Beta, don't worry. I'm coming to Bangalore. I'll reach you tomorrow morning," he consoled him.

Throughout the night he kept awake and prayed. However hard he tried to figure out the reason for the disease, he failed to understand. He couldn't recollect any instance wherein he had unsafe sex or blood transfusion. Despite temptations of a big city, he had lived a virtuous life, and wondered why

God had chosen to cut short his life. With great difficulty he managed a catnap in bits and pieces.

Day Three

Next morning his father arrived when he was still in bed. The old man asked nothing and sought no explanations. Anant was his eldest child and the old man was too shocked to ask his son anything. He asked Anant to pack his belongings and move with him to Shimoga. Before leaving for home Anant took leave of his employers. He lied to them about his illness thinking that they would never learn about it. But he had forgotten that as a routine matter the hospital authorities had informed his employers and parents about his illness and within a few days they would know about it.

He wasn't surprised that none of his friends had called on him in his apartment the previous day. It hurt him the most when Shikha didn't answer his calls. Thought that a similar fate, akin to an ordinary AIDS patient, awaited him, made him shudder.

The journey for them was a long and painful one. They shared nothing except lengthy silences and stolen glances. Neither of them knew how to break the ice and resume talks. Both were too devastated to speak anything and prayed that their agonizing trip got over soon. And when the father saw the first circle outside his hometown, he was relieved. A few minutes later they stepped inside the house. The servant carried their luggage. His mother ran and hugged him, and started crying. He had no words to comfort her. His sisters, Neha and Sweta, and brother, Vishal came running to him and demanded their quota of chocolates, which he fished out of his pocket and handed them over.

Day Four

Alone in bed, he sweated during the night thinking of his imminent death. The night suit, the bed sheet and the pillow covers were all soaked in thick, smelly sweat. In the morning he took a bath, changed the bed seat and pillow covers, and then lay on the bed looking at the blank ceiling. Then he thought of calling Shikha but abandoned the idea, as he didn't want to disturb her in sleep. Instead, he got up, made tea and returned to the bedroom.

He tried to sink his sorrow in the old Hindi songs but to no avail. He couldn't take his mind off her. She was the girl whom he had loved with his heart and soul. How she could leave him when he needed her the most? After about two hours he called her but there was no answer. He called her again and again, still there was no answer. An excruciating pain clove his heart into two.

Was she evading his calls deliberately? He pondered.

And he could have kept thinking about it had his mother not called for breakfast. He dragged his feet to the dining room and sat at the table. Seated in a corner, he ate little and didn't bother to wait for his parents to finish. He got up and came back to his room.

His world turned upside down when his aunt arrived unannounced before lunch. She was closeted with his mother for a long time. And when she came out things changed for him for the worse. The old woman had poisoned his mother's ears and changed the mind of a simple soul.

It shocked him when the maid served the lunch in the bedroom. So, his isolation had begun at home. He said nothing to anyone. There was no use to question his parents about it. They were human beings and acting as per the dictates of their wisdom. It would have caused him more pain if he had argued with them about it. Though he wished not to know what his family members thought about his illness, destiny had the other plans. In the afternoon he walked into the kitchen to get a glass of water when he heard his mother instruct the maidservant to keep his plate, glass and bowls separately in the corner and not mix them up with other utensils.

His heart sank. Immediately he returned to the room and brooded over his uncertain future. Depressed, he called Shikha but failed to get any response from her. She wasn't picking up her cell phone. He felt she had slipped out of his life, perhaps forever. Was there any point in contacting her? He pondered and hung up.

Slowly his friends stopped calling him. Even those who had met him the day he had left the hospital and promised to call him up had not lived up to their promise. Some of them whom he had rung up hadn't bothered to call back. Then it sunk in his mind that nobody would keep in touch with an AIDS patient. He had become a social pariah for everyone, for his friends, fiancée and relatives, who had learned about his illness despite the best efforts by his family to keep it a secret. Another long day in his life had crawled by. As usual he had dinner in his room and he ate little. His mother came and reminded him to take the medicines. Her teary eyes said it all.

He tried to drown his sorrows into the books and magazines but didn't succeed. Later he gazed in the dark outside for a long time before falling off to sleep.

Day Five

Anant woke up late the next morning. He dressed up and ate breakfast, brought by the maidservant. Thereafter, he paced to and fro in the balcony. Loneliness had become his constant companion. He had no one to talk to, no one to share his grief with. The family members avoided him. Except his mother and the maidservant, no one came in his room. Neha, Sweta and Vishal didn't bother to see him. Perhaps, father had told them to keep a safe distance from him. He wanted to talk with them, play with them. When the isolation became unbearable, he came out of his room and joined them in the drawing-room. They were playing the carom.

"Bhaiya, come. We need you to complete the foursome," an excited Neha spoke.

"Please," others pleaded.

"All right," he said forcing a smile on his grim face and joined them in the game.

After about ten minutes he heard his father's footsteps in the corridor. Unmindful, he continued to play and was shocked to hear his father yell at them, "Neha, Sweta, Vishal. Go back to your rooms."

"Papa, please let us play," they begged.

"No. Bhaiya is sick. Let him take rest. Don't disturb him," he argued.

"But he looks OK," Vishal objected.

"Don't argue. Do as I say."

The old man's menacing looks sent them away. His eyes followed them until the door closed. Then he turned to Anant. A pleasing demeanour replaced his frown. He went to him and asked, "Beta, how are you?"

"I'm fine, Papa," a confused Anant mumbled trying to find out the true feeling his father had for him that moment.

"Why are you putting on the Band-Aid?" his father looked worried.

"Papa, in the morning I was trying to prune the rose plants and I injured my thumb but don't worry, it's a minor cut. It will heal soon," he spoke in a quiet tone.

"Anant, you should take care of yourself. From now on you won't do gardening. Please stay in your bedroom," the father said.

Anant nodded.

"Beta, they are kids but you are an intelligent man and hence you should be careful. Your injury can be serious for others in the family," he heard his father complain.

"Ji Papa," he said and walked back to his room.

After lunch he had a good sleep, induced by the medicines. When he got up in the evening he found a new TV lying in the bedroom. His first reaction was of joyful surprise but later it anguished him to learn the reason from the servant, who told him that TV was put in his room so that other children could be kept at a safe distance from him. Firstly, the food in the room and then TV, his isolation was now complete.

He sank deep into the sea of despair. By nature he couldn't stay without friends for more than a second and now he was to live alone within the confines of a ten by twelve room. It dawned on him that he was wanted no more in this world. His fiancée had left him. His friends had deserted him. His family tolerated him, perhaps praying for a quick end to his miseries.

In the emptiness of the night he wondered whether the life was at all worth living any longer. He wished it to end soon and if it didn't then perhaps one day he would end it himself. And he felt that day approaching soon. Like the previous nights, he wept in the absolute darkness with tears falling on the bed sheet in a steady stream. On earlier occasions in Bangalore, Shikha had wiped his tears, held him in her arms and comforted him. Now he had nobody to console him. He was too weak to wipe his tears.

With wet eyes, he curled up like a child and tried to sleep. Another day had passed off in his life.

Day Six

Next day's morning was lonelier and more depressing. He had to undergo the same monotonous routine with nothing to look forward to. After a tasteless breakfast, he switched on TV and surfed channels. Since the doctor had broken the sad news to him in the hospital, everything he ate tasted insipid. In fact, he had lost the zest and lived a listless life. Mornings in particular were depressing after nightlong brooding. He contemplated of suicide when his phone rang. It was his sixth day and no one had called up since he had left Bangalore. It might be Shikha; he thought and picked up the phone.

"Hello, Shikha," he said in choked voice.

"Is it Mr. Anant?" the caller was a woman, but it wasn't her voice. He was disappointed but recovered soon, and replied, "Yeah, Ma'am."

"Mr. Anant, I'm Sanjeevani. I work in a NGO called 'Jyoti'. We work with the AIDS patients and help them to live a dignified life in the society, which is so ignorant about the disease. I want to meet you. Can I come today?"

He heard her patiently. It gave him a few moments of joy that somebody was coming to meet him. His instant reply was, "Yes ma'am, you can come anytime. I've nothing much to do except wait for death."

"Mr. Anant, don't lose hope. I'll be there in a few hours' time with something positive for you," he heard her say and then the click sound signalled the end of their short conversation.

His wait got longer with each passing minute and when she didn't turn up until after lunch, he began to lose hope. He thought it a prank by a sick person. What could he do than curse his luck? After all, the fate had played the biggest prank on him. He was about to doze off when the doorbell rang. He ran out to open the door and was surprised to see a beautiful girl standing outside.

"Are you Sanjeevani?" he asked.

"Yeah. Will you let me in or ask everything here?" she smiled.

"Oh, I'm so sorry," he apologized realizing his mistake and then ushered her in his room.

"Sanjeevani," she said again extending her hand in a formal introduction.

With reluctance he put his hand forward. She gave him a warm handshake. It was so assuring, the first one in almost a week. They sat on the chairs. He offered her water.

"Mr. Anant, I ....," she was about to begin when he interrupted her, "Please, call me Anant."

"Well Anant, I learned about you through our network spanning across the country. I fully sympathize with you. Don't lose hope. There's a lot of life, good and meaningful, to live as AIDS patient and we, I mean our organization, Jyoti, works with the AIDS patients to realize that dream," she spoke and paused to get his response.

He saw the dark clouds disappear from the horizon and a ray of hope emanate from a small corner. Her words sounded like that of a gospel. He looked at her in hope, in faith and tears rolled down his misty eyes. Wiping tears, he said, "Sanjeevani, you've brought a new hope in my gloomy life."

She said nothing but gave him a long, assuring look. It had a mesmerizing effect on him. Before her sat a shattered man who had lost all hopes and needed her support. For a few moments they shared a studied silence. He needed it to regain faith in himself, in life.

Then she said, "Anant, do you know about eight million people are suffering from this disease in India and most of them are poor and illiterate people whose knowledge about the disease is based on hearsay than facts. Awareness about the disease among them is low and that is the cause of concern for all of us. To top it all, they face humiliation and social ostracism from everyone—their families, their friends and their doctors, who are too afraid to treat them for the fear of contacting disease."

"Now I know the educated lot is no better. I suffer the same humiliation each day here in my home," the behavior of his parents had made him bitter.

"Since you are going through the similar experience, may I request you to share yours with other patients? That would give them a lot of confidence and hope that their world—the poor man's world—is not the only bad world. The rich people too meet the similar fate."

"Isn't it ironic that the deadliest disease known to humanity is bridging the social divide," he remarked.

She smiled. Then she heard his entire story with compassion. He narrated at length and told her about his friends, Shikha and his family, and how each one of them had abandoned him midstream.

"It's unfortunate but it happens with almost every AIDS patient," was her refrain. "It's surprising that even educated people don't behave well with them. I read in the morning paper that the AIDS victims are denied proper burial space in Kottayam and being buried in the condemned graves meant for people who do not live their lives according to the religious teachings. A wall separated the condemned graves from rest of the cemetery. Following protests led by Sister Dolores and others, the wall was pulled down. So, you see, we still have a long way to go."

"Wait, I'll get you tea," he stood up.

She gestured him to stay seated and said, "No, thanks. I'll have next time. Now I should leave and return to my patients at Jyoti. Hope you are coming tomorrow."

He nodded and saw her off at the gate. She shook hands and said, "Cheer up." He watched her go.

Sanjeevani's visit pepped him up. His mood changed to optimism and he spent his remaining day in peace.

Day Seven

Next day he was up before daybreak. He got ready, put on new clothes and went to Jyoti, at the other end of the city. Sanjeevani greeted her there. After a brief tour of the place he was taken to a big hall where a large gathering waited for him. From the podium he surveyed the crowd present. Most of them were poor people, coming from the lower and semi-literate sections of the society. Their shabby clothes depicted the state of their minds. He looked around for some cheerful faces in the gathering but found none. They all seemed to wait for death.

In the college he wasn't considered a glib talker leave alone addressing a huge crowd suffering from a terminal disease. Motivating them was hard because he knew he didn't possess great persuasive skills. He decided to share his honest feeling with them, since the day he had learned about disease and how people around him, including those who loved him so much, had changed so suddenly.

He recollected his thoughts, composure and spoke. Throughout speech the audience remained spellbound and when he finished, they greeted him with misty eyes and thunderous applause. Some of them approached him and shared their sorrows and hurt. He consoled them all like a seasoned healer.

The experience humbled him. Spontaneity of their emotions overwhelmed him and rekindled love for life. From a yard she watched him mingle with patients in the crowd. He had a natural flair for motivating masses. She wondered whether he could join Jyoti and show the light to thousands of AIDS patients who lived in darkness and hopelessness.

Once the crowd melted away, she came and said, "Anant, you've great persuasive skills. Have you noticed their faces? They had grim faces when they came in here but now they have left with smiles. I'm so happy you spoke to them."

"I'm happy to share my feelings with them. This trip has been worth it," his mood was buoyant.

They had tea together, after which they took a stroll around the place. She apprised him of the efforts Jyoti was making with the AIDS patients in Karnataka. He was impressed by her dedication and sincerity in taking up a social cause at such a young age, when the most girls of her age took up a job and lived a cushy life.

"Sanjeevani, person like you make me feel small and selfish," Anant said.

"I'm doing nothing exceptional, just following my conscious," she was humble.

"I want to join your organization and help the folks here," he said.

"Why not, you can join us anytime," Sanjeevani beamed.

It was getting late and he expressed his wish to return home. She escorted him to the gate and saw him off. Half-hour later he was back in the bedroom, alone. Today's visit had kindled a ray of hope in his heart and given him reason to live whatever days were left of his life. Like Sanjeevani, he too would devote his life in the service of the AIDS victims, he decided.

That night he ate well and slept in peace.

Next day till noon his routine remained usual. In the afternoon a courier arrived. It surprised him that someone still thought of sending letter to him. Who could he or she be? He thought and opened the envelope.

It was a letter from the Leela Nursing Home. He read it. The second blood report, which they had sent to a different laboratory, said he was HIV negative. The report had a letter attached to it. Dr Kesarvani had wished him well for a happy, normal life.

For a moment he stood motionless, unable to react to his medical report. He didn't know whether to laugh or cry. In the last seven days he had been through hell and his emotional reservoir had dried up. The eyes had stoned and heart had become one long empty desert.

It was the happiest news of his life and he wanted to share it with someone special. He rang up Sanjeevani and told her about it. For a moment he heard nothing from her. Then her soft sobs rang in his ears followed by heavy resonance of her cries. He felt the tup, tup sounds of her tears falling in the mouthpiece. And then he heard her say, "Anant wait, I'm coming."

It was the longest wait of his life. And when the doorbell rang, he ran to receive her. Without bothering about anyone, she hugged him at the doorstep and said, "Congratulations. God has given you a new life."

They moved into his bedroom where he showed her his second blood report. In surprise she burst out laughing and tears of joy rolled down her cheeks. Her tears stirred his heart in which emotions resurfaced. They cried together, smiled together.

"I'm so happy for you, Anant. Now you can go back to your world. I mean to your parents, friends and Shikha," she said, wiping eyes.

He gazed in her eyes and said with a shrug, "No. I don't belong to their world. They don't need me. In fact, no one from my past needs me. These seven days have shown me the true face of the world. After visiting Jyoti yesterday I've decided that I belong to those unfortunate people. My world is with them, it's with you. I hope you won't turn me away from Jyoti."

"Who would turn such a wonderful person away? It's my good luck you'll join us," she spoke with a lump in her throat.

She wished him well and returned home. Later he told his parents who hugged him and wept. Their behaviour was surprising. For the last seven days they had avoided talking to him, leave alone giving him an assuring pat. He knew he was in for more surprises.

Next he called up Shikha's parents who were glad to hear the news. They told him that Shikha would come with them to see him in the evening. When his friends learned about his second report, they came running and took turns to shake hands with him, hug him and wish him well. They were euphoric and ecstatic. His friends, his parents' friends and their well-wishers thronged the house. They all wished him good luck.

Now the atmosphere in the house had changed and so had the people around him. For seven long days he had lived a lonely existence with nobody to share his grief with. While others celebrated the good news, he remained lost in thoughts and pondered his future course of action.

He was still in a pensive mood when his father walked up to him and said, "Beta, Shikha's parents called me a few minutes ago. They will come in the evening to discuss and finalize the date of your marriage. They favour advancing the date."

Amused, he looked at him, but said nothing. Now the things were moving so fast in his life. Speed of occurrence of the events scared him. Slowness of the past week had taught him the life's many lessons and cleared the cobwebs in his mind. Paved with flowers a new path now waited for him to begin his journey.

In the evening Shikha came with her parents and hugged him in a visible display of her affection. As the elders went to the drawing-room, she pulled him in the bedroom where she hugged him and then filled his face with her hot breath and wet kisses. Like a statue he stood still and felt the outpourings of her emotions. After sometime they joined the elders.

Throughout the talks among the family members he kept quiet. Both the parents agreed for 20th of next month for marriage. After sometime Shikha with her parents left but not before giving him a hug again.

Amused and baffled, he had watched the day's proceedings. He felt like laughing at their bizarre behavior. Before he fell ill people around him were so positive, so full of life. His weeklong illness had brought out the true faces hidden behind the masks. The same folks, who had filled his life with abundance of love, had shunned him when he was suffering from AIDS. Their behaviour had devastated him, but during those dark days Shikha's absence had shredded his heart into pieces. As he lay in bed, pondering over the week gone by, she called up and spoke with him for a long time. In between he uttered 'yeahs', but said nothing. She thought he was recovering from the shock and so she didn't pester him. After a while she said good night and hung up.

Next day Anant dropped the bombshell. When his mother came to wake him up she didn't find him in bed. She looked for him in the bathroom and then ran around the house, but he was nowhere. Then she came back to his bedroom and her gaze fell on a piece of paper, lying on the bedside table.

She read it:

Dear Papa and Mummy,

I'm going to join Jyoti, a NGO, working in the state for the welfare of the AIDS patients. I'll not marry Shikha. Please tell her parents. I won't stay here in this house, but I'll keep coming.

Yours,

Anant

The letter struck her like a lightning. She shouted for her husband who rushed to her. He was shocked to go through the note.

"We deserved it," he said, taking her in his arms.

They knew they would have to shed tears for a long, long time for their mistakes.

Last Bus To Lekhapani

Pooran Mal Lakhotia got down from the paddle rickshaw at the Dibrugarh Bus Station at about 9 p.m. After paying up he rushed to the booking window from where a dim light emanated. It was closed. Disappointed, he looked around for someone to ask about the bus. His gaze stopped at a dull corner where a man was making tea. He picked up the suitcase and went to the teashop. Smell of the boiling tea and rising steam from the blackened pan filled his heart with a strong urge for hot tea. The Brahmaputra night was wrapped in the blanket of cold.

He put down the luggage and rubbed his palms vigorously, blowing into them in between. After a few minutes he asked the tea seller "Bhaiya, what time the bus leaves for Lekhapani?"

The shopkeeper gave him a wry smile and said, "Sahib, you've just missed the bus. It has left a half-hour ago."

"When is the next one?" he asked.

"The last bus leaves at midnight. The booking counter will open fifteen minutes before that. Few passengers travel by the last bus," he replied.

"What time does the bus reach Lekhapani?"

"About 4 a.m."

"4 a.m.!"

"Ji Sahib. It seems you are coming here for the first time. In this region the sun rises early. It's dawn by 4 a.m."

"What's your name?"

"Lallan."

"Lallan, can I've a strong ginger tea?" he asked.

"Hahn, Sahib. Wait a minute," he dusted a plastic chair with his *gamchha* and then gestured him to sit.

"I'll spend time here at the bus stop. There's no point going back to the hotel room now," he said, settling in the chair.

"Sahib, you won't regret it," he heard him remark.

"Why!" he exclaimed.

"Ji, nothing. I mean you can read the book or newspaper. You would be carrying a lot of books," he said, putting tea leaves in the boiling water.

"How do you know?" Pooran asked in surprise.

"I've seen many sahibs reading books waiting for the bus." he put sugar in the pan and stirred it. A minute later when the tea started to boil, he chopped a ginger into fine pieces and dropped them in the pan.

"Do you know how to read?" Pooran asked, but felt foolish a minute later for such a stupid question.

He watched the tea seller's every action minutely. Lallan searched for an unbroken cup from the pile, washed it with water and then wiped it with the clean *gamchha*.

"Ji, sahib. I've attended the school till class V. Thereafter I left it because my father couldn't afford it. He asked me to help him in the shop," he stirred tea, strained it and then poured it in the cup and handed to him.

"Thanks."

"How's the tea?" the seller asked, anticipating a nice compliment.

"Quite refreshing. Thank you so much," was Pooran's genuine reaction. "It's the best tea since I landed in India."

Pooran had seen Lallan take great pains in making tea for him and serve it in the best cup. His eyes became moist thinking of the respect tea seller gave him.

Taking a sip, he asked, "Lallan, you don't look an Assamese. Where's your home town?"

"Sahib, your guess is correct. I'm from Buxor in Bihar. About fifty years ago my parents had come to this place looking for the job and they settled down here. I was born in Dibrugarh."

"Have you ever been to Buxor?"

"Ji. Thrice. When my father was alive he took us there once in five years. He had some land that he sold off during his last visit."

"Where is he now?"

"He died last year. My mother had died a year before him. Now I'm alone with my wife and three children."

"Do you ever feel like going back to your native place? I mean Buxor."

"Sometimes I do. This place always seems *pardesh* to me, though I was born here. The local people look down upon us. They treat us as outsiders. Often we bear the brunt of their wrath when ethnic violence erupts in the area," his voice was sad and mood reflective.

"I understand your difficulty," he empathized. "I guess people would keep migrating in search of jobs within or outside their states and countries."

Sadness in Lallan's voice was gone and he asked, "Sahib, are you from Delhi?"

"No. I'm coming from Atlanta," he answered and then realized the poor man wouldn't know where Atlanta was. So, he added as an afterthought, "America."

"Oh, America. Sahib, I heard there are no beggars or poor people in that country," he spoke in excitement.

"The majority of Americans are rich," he said. There was no point in telling Lallan about the poor and homeless people in the Unites States, and break his heart. Most Indians carried a rosy picture of America in their minds.

"So, what are you doing there, sahib?"

"I've a business."

"I've heard Indian businessmen earn a lot of money there. You would be a rich man."

"Hmm."

Lallan looked at him and said, "Sahib, you've plenty of money. Why didn't you hire a taxi?"

"Yeah, you're right. In the morning I had asked the hotel manager to get me a taxi but he advised against it. He told me the United Liberation Front of Assam (ULFA) targetted the rich businessmen. Hence, travelling by taxi was unsafe."

"The manager gave you the right advice. The ULFA is all over the place. Travelling alone isn't safe in this part of the state. Bus is a better option but you should have taken the day bus."

"Yeah, but during day I was busy in sorting out my business problems and I didn't get time. I was afraid I might not get the telephone and Internet facilities in Lekhapani."

Lallan couldn't understand what Pooran said but he nodded nonetheless, "Ji, sahib. Lekhapani is a small place. I've been there once when I worked on the road construction."

"Why did you come back from there?" Pooran asked.

"What could I do? When the road was completed I had to return home."

"Can you tell me something about that place?"

"I'm sorry I can't recollect much. I worked there ten years ago. Moreover, I didn't see the town. We lived in the makeshift shelters half-mile away from the city. We visited the Sunday market once a week to buy the groceries."

"OK, don't mind. I'll find out when I reach there tomorrow."

The night was getting chillier as the Tibet wind, rolling down from the Himalayas, had picked up speed. Pooran rubbed his palms vigorously to beat the cold. Hearing the cluttering of his teeth, Lallan lit his *bhutthi* (the earthen stove) and Pooran pulled his chair closer to the flames.

"Sahib, it's got cold. Should I get you a blanket?"

"*Nahin, Shukriya.* My jacket is warm and this *bhutthi* is giving me good heat."

"Sahib, may I ask you something?"

"*Hahn.*"

"What brings you to this desolate place? Who's there in Lekhapani?"

"Oh Lekhapani! My uncle lives there. Since past one month he isn't well. I got the news that he is serious. So, I'm here to look him up."

"What's his name?"

"Why? Do you know any business person there?" Pooran probed.

"No, I asked just like that," Lallan uttered.

"Kirori Mal Lakhotia."

"I've heard about him. He is a rich man and owns many tea gardens. He lives in a big haveli in the town, has a fleet of cars and a dozen servants. Alas! He has no children."

"Yeah, that's unfortunate. I'm his closet relative. Do you know when he came here; he had a few hundred rupees in the pocket. Now I believe he is a *crorepati*."

"His meteoric rise to name and fame has become folklore among the local population, in particular the non-Assamese who draw a lot of inspiration from him. He has shown us that if one works hard then one can do anything in life," Lallan's eyes glowed in admiration.

Pooran was delighted to hear him praise his uncle, though the truth only he knew. The old man never gave a dime to the dying man. In his native place Kirori Mal was infamous for being a miser. And he was sure his uncle wouldn't have changed now. In the village the old man didn't have much wealth except vast acres of arid land, which yielded no crops. But the man was obsessed with business and making money.

Their small village in Jhunjhunu district was famous for two things. One, it sent a large number of young men to the Indian army. Two, its traders did a flourishing business outside the state, mostly in Calcutta. And those businessmen when they returned home displayed their wealth. They built huge houses, which remained locked for the entire year except for a fortnight when they visited the village during the Diwali festival.

So, the villagers looked at those mansions in awe and jealousy. Kirori Mal too had grown up admiring those huge houses and aspired to build his own. He was driven by the passion to earn money, which, he knew, could only be earned outside the state. While the most fortune seekers headed towards Calcutta in West Bengal, he opted for Assam. Before him no other trader had ventured that far for the fear of the tribes. When he left the village he had a few hundred rupees in his pocket. With his indomitable will he started his business in a new and alien place. In the beginning, he faced a lot of hardships but later he succeeded and earned a lot of money.

"Sahib, what happened?"

"Nothing. I was recollecting my childhood."

"You are remembering your uncle. He would have raised you with a lot of love and affection."

"*Hahn*. He did," the nostalgia filled his heart. In front of a stranger he didn't want to belittle his ailing uncle but in his heart he carried many unpleasant memories. During childhood he had struggled to study in good schools and then stand on his feet. And he had achieved that with little help from his uncle.

With determination he had made it big in the export business in India and later migrated to the United States. But somehow his luck had deserted him there and he had incurred huge losses in the business. He alone knew the true financial health of his company. For ten years he had lived abroad and visited his uncle once in their native village, where the extended family had gathered for his cousin's marriage. During his stay in India he had clicked well with uncle who had invited him to visit Lekhapani.

Pooran's busy schedule had kept him away from India for long but in the intervening period he had been in constant touch with his uncle through letters. And when he received a phone call from his uncle's doctor, he rushed back to India.

In ten years the fate had turned a full circle. While he was on the brink of insolvency, his uncle had become a millionaire. And he had hoped uncle to bail him out of the financial mess he had landed himself into. On the phone the doctor had hinted that his uncle wasn't going to live long and he had signed a new will. Pooran had hoped to get a part of his uncle's wealth, if not whole property.

He looked at the watch. It was 11 p.m. Lifting the collar of his jacket; he pulled up the chain till his neck and wrapped a muffler around his head, covering his ears and mouth. The wind had got chillier and stronger.

"Lallan, I'll have another tea," he said.

He already had drunk four cups in the past one hour to fight the cold but in vain. The air was frigorific. With every passing minute the chill seeped deeper into his bones. Through a small opening in the muffler he saw Lallan make tea. When the hot tea trickled down the esophagus, he felt the warmth spread to all parts of the body. It tasted good and gave him much needed heat. He thanked Lallan for it.

"Wish I had anticipated this, then I would have taken the day bus," he rued his decision of taking the night bus.

"Don't worry, sahib. It's a matter of an hour," Lallan told him.

Pooran's legs had begun to ache. He stood up and walked about the place for a few minutes before returning to the chair. "I hope the journey is hassle free," he sighed.

"Sure it would be, but be careful," Lallan cautioned.

"Why? Is there any danger en route?" a worried Pooran asked.

"I've heard some strange things about the night bus."

"Like?"

"Last week a passenger told me that he had a dreadful encounter with a ghost in the bus."

Pooran laughed aloud and mocked, "You believed him."

"Sahib, I haven't seen the ghosts but my father told me he had escaped once from their clutches. So, I guess they do exist. I've no reason to disbelieve my father," he replied.

Pooran had no intention to debate with him on the existence of ghosts. So he kept quiet and waited for him to continue. His silence was taken as admission of his belief.

"Sahib, people say the night journey is fraught with dangers. Weird things happen in the bus. A week ago an old man narrated how somebody robbed him at the midnight when he had dozed off in the bus for a few minutes. And two days ago a passenger told me that in the night he saw a man on the road waving at the driver to stop, but the conductor urged the driver not to look out and speed up the bus. On reaching Lekhapani he told everybody that the man waving at the bus wasn't a human being but a ghost."

"How do you know all this?" Pooran was getting interested.

A baffled Lallan replied, "Sahib, I get to hear them because the passengers narrate their experiences to me and to others over a cup of tea at my shop."

"So, you are privy to several tales of the night bus," he smiled.

"Ji," Lallan blushed and continued, "Other day an Assamese told me that he would get a big fortune within a fortnight. His wealthy employer was going to bequeath his entire property to him."

"That's called luck," Pooran remarked.

"No sahib. It's a reward for his twenty years of dedicated service to his master, the man told me."

"What reward? No master gives his life's earnings to his servant. He gives it to his children or to the relatives or donates it to any charitable trust. It's weird and unbelievable," Pooran shrugged.

"Maybe sahib what you say is true, but the man sounded convincing to me. I pray he gets the fortune," Lallan was happy that a poor man was about to get the fortune. At least a guy his like him would be a rich man someday.

Pooran was eager to know the name of the businessman who was about to bequeath his property to a total stranger leaving his children in the lurch. Turning to Lallan he asked, "Did the servant tell you the name of his master?"

Engrossed in talks with the tea seller, he didn't notice the bus had wheeled in and people were boarding it. The conductor was waiting for some passengers pissing on the wall in a dark corner. The driver honked repeatedly to draw their attention.

Lallan heard the honks. He picked up the suitcase and said, "Sahib, the bus is about to leave. Let's hurry up."

Forgetting the question, Pooran rushed and got inside the bus, followed by Lallan who put the suitcase in the luggage rack. Then he spoke with misty eyes, "Sahib, if you happen to return by bus, please don't forget to have tea at my shop."

"Sure," Pooran said, shaking hands.

Lallan got down and stood by the widow where Pooran sat. And when the last passenger boarded the driver moved out. Lallan ran a few steps with the bus and then spoke in a loud voice, "Sahib, I can recollect now. The servant told me that his master's name was ..." The rest got drowned in the sounds of screeches and honks.

The tea seller halted. The bus picked up speed and vanished in the dark. He came back to his shop, wound it up and went home.

A strange fear gripped Pooran, though he knew that none of his uncles had given away their property in charity or to a stranger. They all had bequeathed their property to their children or relatives. Thus the wealth remained in the hands of the family members. No outsider could ever dream of getting a penny out of their fortunes. Suddenly a doubt crept in his mind: What if his uncle had a change of heart? He didn't want to think about that as it could mean a financial disaster for him. To save his sinking business he had pinned a lot of hopes on his uncle's money.

The most passengers were either fast sleep or dozing off. Undisturbed by snores, he sat awake. The bus moved at a breakneck speed on the mountainous road. Perhaps no passenger had so much to lose in life the next morning. After what Lallan had told him about his uncle he didn't get a wink of sleep. Deep within his heart the suspicion cropped up about his uncle's wisdom. But when he remembered his uncle's nature his confidence returned. On a few occasions in the past Kirori Mal had told the family members that after his death Pooran would carry forward his name and business. It brought a smile on his face.

Lost in uncle's thoughts, he spent the last hour of his journey, dozing off and on. At about 4 a.m. the bus reached the destination. He got down. Several rickshaw pullers encircled him and asked where he wanted to go. After haggling with them he chose a rickshaw and moved to his uncle's house. Lekhapani was a small, sleepy town caught in a time warp where life moved at a snail's pace. On either of the road were the tea gardens. The mud plastered bamboo houses with rusted tin roofs and bamboo cattle fences passed by at regular intervals. Tambul trees adored the front and backyards of every small or big house. The countryside wore a pastoral look. As he approached the city centre the clogged open drains in front of the houses told the story of the governmental neglect and apathy. Only change since his last visit was presence of the gun-carrying soldiers at important city intersections. The roadside shops were opening up. The egg sellers, meat sellers and vegetable sellers were busy in arranging their shops.

The town was too small to accommodate the ambitions of a modern man. He wondered how his uncle had stayed in that place for so long and managed to create so much wealth. Could a modern man stay there forever if someone paid him a million dollar for that? He wondered. The rickshaw puller knew his uncle and so he reached there without any hassles. A servant took him inside the huge bungalow. Putting the luggage in corridor he rushed to his uncle's bedroom. The doctor waited by the bedside of the ailing Kirori Mal.

He called out, "*Chachaji,*" seeing his uncle lying on the bed but got no response. He went closer and looked at him. The old man lay still on his favourite bed. When Kirori Mal saw Pooran his lips quivered but the voice failed him. The patient's face had a surprised look. Pooran took uncle's hand in his and pressed and then felt the grip tightening. He peeped in the old misty eyes. A couple of tears trickled down the sunken cheeks. A strong feeling of guilt seized him for neglecting uncle and failing to see the love the old man had for him. After a while he felt a hand on the shoulder.

Doctor Mishra took Pooran aside and said in sad tone, "He won't survive the weekend. You are the closest relative he had, so I called you to do his last rites. Your uncle had told me that Saikia should light his pyre if you didn't turn up."

"Saikia, who?"

"He is the manager in whom Mr. Kirori Mal has a blind faith. In fact, he trusts Saikia more than anybody else. But I believe that either the son or a family member should do his last rites because then only his soul will be liberated from this world."

"Doctor, you are a well-meaning man. Thank you so much for calling me here," he said.

"Take rest. You look tired," the doctor said and then whispered after initial hesitation, "There is one more thing I need to tell you. I heard the rumour that Sethji wanted to give everything to Saikia. That was before he wrote his last will."

Pooran watched him make a hasty exit. Later the servant showed him his bedroom. He went to the toilet, got ready and appeared after an hour in the dining room for breakfast. Outside in the drawing-room he found an Assamese man waiting for him.

"Sorry, I couldn't meet you in the morning. I'm Saikia, the manager," he extended his hand.

Pooran shook hands and exchanged a few pleasantries with him. He heard someone call out for Saikia who begged leave of him. Alone in the room he contemplated about his future course of action. In the front courtyard the swing hanging under the guava tree drew his attention. He came out and touched the wooden plank, weathered by years of rain, wind and sun. Flooded with childhood memories he caught hold of the rope.

Many summers ago when he had stayed with uncle for a week he had planted the mango, guava and Gulmohar trees. He recollected his uncle, sitting in the recliner in veranda; tell him, "Pooran, the man who nurtures the tree gets to eat its fruit."

Next day the servant gave him morning tea with the sad news of his uncle's demise. He put on his slippers and ran out. The entire household had gathered there. Some people were inside the house, while others waited outside. Wading through the crowd he entered the room and saw the doctor at the bedside.

"Pooran, Sethji died at dawn due to cardiac arrest. You can cremate him in the evening after the post-mortem," The doctor stood up and gave a pat on his shoulder.

Saikia organized everything. Before the sunset his uncle's body was laid on the pyre and the panditji called for Pooran to do the puja. In front of a large crowd he lit the pyre. The wood pile smouldered, but when the panditji poured a few tins of *desi ghee*, it sent out tall flames that threatened to touch the sky.

Standing alone in the corner Pooran watched the golden flames consume his uncle's frail body. His eyes filled up. At last he had managed to shed tears for his uncle. He felt relieved, he felt human. After collecting the ashes Saikia and he returned to the haveli. They walked in complete silence. He wanted the rituals to get over soon so that he could return home to his wife and children. But he had to stay there till other mandatory rituals were over.

A day after '*Tehravin*' a small group of people, comprising the witnesses in whose presence Kirori Mal had signed his last will, gathered. The family lawyer checked if all were present in the house. Assured, he opened the envelope and began to read.

Pooran couldn't tolerate the suspense and presumed that nothing was for him in that will; he slipped out of the room. Seconds later the lawyer pursued him. He called out from behind, "Listen, Mr. Pooran. Wait. Don't go away. I've something important to tell you."

Pooran heard someone shout for him. He stopped, turned back and walked towards the lawyer.

"Mr. Pooran, Your uncle has bequeathed his entire property to you."

"What!" Pooran couldn't believe it.

"Yeah," the lawyer nodded. "You heard me right. But he has left a rider. You'll have to stay in Lekhapani forever to get his fortune and you can't sell it."

"What if I don't stay here?" he sought clarification.

"In that case Saikia gets it all."

Twins

After doing B Tech from IT Roorkee, Vikas wanted to do MBA like most of his colleagues but somewhere in the midway he lost steam for hard work and instead settled for a well-paying job in one of the multi-nationals that had thronged India consequent to recession in the Silicon Valley.

Whether Vikas's company had employed him on a low salary or he had grabbed a well-paying job, was a moot question that often troubled him for some time until he got an emotional call from his ailing mother. She wanted him to get married soon so that she could play with the grandchildren before she breathed her last. And whenever she tried to blackmail him emotionally, his response was, "Mummy, you will live a thousand years and get to play with your great-grandchildren too."

Vikas knew he couldn't convince her however hard he tried. She wouldn't survive for more than a couple of years. Though the family had tried to keep her terminal illness a secret from her, she had learned about it somehow. And that explained her eagerness to get her son married soon.

Earlier he had argued with her that until he got a well-paying job he wouldn't marry but now the situation was different. Moreover, he didn't wish to disappoint her. He loved her so much that he couldn't cause her any pain. If it were for her happiness he prepared himself mentally to marry soon to see smile on her gloomy face. And so when he told her on the phone that he was willing to get married, for a moment he got no response from the other side. Afraid, he called out, “Mummy, what happened?”

Her voice was preceded by the familiar sobs and perhaps wiping of tears, of happiness, from the *pallo* of her sari, “*Munna,* I can’t tell how happy I’m. You’ve fulfilled my longstanding wish, my last dream. Now I can die in peace after seeing my daughter-in-law’s face. Tell me who’s your dream girl? I’ll ask your papa to fix up the marriage within a month.”

Perhaps she had stopped crying because she spoke her last sentence without hiccups. Vikas took time to compose his response, “Mummy, I’m not seeing any girl. I would like you to choose the girl for me.”

He heard her distinct broken laughter. Perhaps she hadn’t believed him. He strained ears to hear her say, amidst giggles, “*Munna,* come on, don’t tell me you’ve no girlfriend. I don’t believe it. You are smarter than your Papa. Even he, thirty-five years ago, had a girlfriend.”

“Who was she?” asked Vikas.

For a few seconds there was total silence. Then he heard her coy voice, “Me.”

Overjoyed, he imagined that her mother’s cheeks that moment would be rosy and dimples red. He missed the opportunity to see her blushing.

“Mummy, I’m lucky you chose me to share your tender secret. But believe me, I’ve no girlfriend, though it might sound bizarre to you,” he tried to convince her.

“Tell me, what qualities you want in your soulmate?” her voice had become serious.

“She may not be half as beautiful as you, but I want a loving and caring girl? I won’t settle for less,” he said in a serious tone but heard her laughter.

"So, you want me around you when I'm gone," she laughed.

He marvelled at her dexterity, her ability to live life on her terms. She knew she wasn't going to live long, yet she tried to light up her every living moment. But it didn't occur to him that his decision to marry had given her immense joy for a few moments. She agreed to send him the photos and bio-data of a dozen girls.

A week later he received a fat envelope through the courier and when he opened it more than a dozen photos of beautiful girls slipped out of his hands and fell on the bed. They all seemed to stare at him; some faces were serious, some were smiling while others were indifferent. He shuffled through each of them in detail over a cup of coffee, often matching their faces with bio-data. Among those beautiful faces a few girls aroused his curiosity. He shortlisted them and then told his mother about it. She asked him to come home soon to see the girls.

A few days later he landed up at home to the delight of everyone, especially mother who couldn't contain her joy. The same day she saw the photos and bio-data of the girls he had chosen and then sat with her phone for more than an hour and fixed up the meeting with the girls' parents. Next day she went for shopping and purchased half a dozen saris for herself, and showed them to him in the evening. She had enthusiasm of a young woman who was about to wear those saris for the first time. In great details she told him which sari she would wear on what function. Despite his argument that he had many suits already, she bought him a dozen suits. Her logic was that her son should look the handsomest when he went to see the girls.

As usual his amused father watched them from the sidelines and when his eyes got teary he moved away. The old man didn't shed tears in front of her as that could aggravate her health. He was too young to understand what thoughts went on in his father's mind and how would he cope with her loss in future. Vikas had never seen father show his love for her in public, but he knew his father loved his mother so much. Perhaps it was a man's fate to cry in silence. On his shoulders rested the responsibility of the family and he couldn't show his weakness and make others weaker.

Two days later he and his parents went to see the first girl. He had taken care to dress well. Somehow he had this notion that the man had the right to reject, but when the first girl refused to marry him on the pretext that he was old-fashioned, he was crestfallen. Father as usual was calm but mother got furious. She took the rejection to her heart and kept saying, "How dare she reject my handsome son?"

Father and he had great difficulty in pacifying her. An hour later she calmed down and then fixed up the next meeting. The first rejection had taught Vikas one good lesson, which was that even the girls could reject the boys. So, he was better prepared this time. His experience with the next girl wasn't as bad. She was a decent girl who unlike the first one didn't reject him in front of everyone. In fact, she spoke to him alone.

In privacy she bared her heart to him, "Vikas, don't take me wrong. I'm in love with a boy. I want to marry him."

"So, you want me to say no. It's OK," he gave a smile, "Don't worry. I'll do it. At least you rejected me in private. Thanks."

He came out of the room and told everyone that he couldn't marry the girl because both had nothing in common. Without any heartburn to either family they moved out from there. Mother's reaction this time too was hostile, though a bit subdued. After unpleasant experiences with first two girls, Vikas had become more circumspect. In fact, he had steeled himself for any type of setback in future.

Further experiences of seeing girls were hilarious. One girl confessed to him that had she not been in love with someone else, she would have agreed to marry him. She had found him an affable guy. He expressed gratitude to her for her compliments and asked what she expected from him. She said that since she couldn't refuse the proposal herself, she asked him to turn it down. He assured her and came out of the room smiling.

His mother picked up the smile, which he had tried to hide. She took it as a positive signal and her loud sigh echoed in the drawing-room, but when he told them about his decision, he met their angry gazes. Before leaving he slipped a note into the girl's father's hand. It urged him to marry his daughter to the man she loved. Though he had broken many hearts that day, at least he had saved a girl from getting into a loveless matrimony. His mother wasn't happy with his decision, but father was supportive of it.

In coming days a few more girls pleaded him to play the role of a saviour for them. Having gained the expertise, he played that role with aplomb. However, his parents, mother in particular, were far from being pleased. She had begun to despair and never forgot to curse the girls who had rejected her son so far. But somehow she had an inkling of the game her son was playing. She knew he was declining the proposals, not of his volition but at the behest of the girls. To put mother at ease, he told her that it was a matter of time before she would find a beautiful girl as her daughter-in-law. It had the desired effect on her, as the words brought a wide grin on her face. And the afterglow of that smile lingered on until they went to see the next girl.

He began to view the experience as an adventure. It had become one as it contained the elements of almost everything; the drama, suspense, intrigue, hope and anguish. As a matter of fact, he started to enjoy it and looked forward to the next meeting. Perhaps God had planned good things for him. His search for the perfect girl ended one day. The luck smiled on him, out of pity or perhaps a reward for his good work in the past week. They landed up at the house of the Bhargavas and were given a warm welcome, like on the previous occasions.

The guests held back their breath when they heard some hush-hush in the air, heralding arrival of the girl. Dressed in a Banarasi silk sari, she walked in and did namaste to everybody. Vikas looked at his mother whose heart, it seemed, the girl had won over. Mother asked her, "Sanjana, *beta* come, sit beside me."

He saw her move like a doll and sit next to his mother on the sofa. Both exchanged a few affectionate glances and then mother asked her some questions to clear her misgivings. In the meanwhile his father talked with her parents while he sat as an onlooker. In between he gave one-word answers to the questions thrown at him by the girl's parents.

Then two servants arrived with tea, sweets and snacks. They placed the trays on the glass table. Mrs. Bhargava leaned and poured tea into the cups. Then she handed one cup to everyone. Mr. Bhargava did the duty of showing them snacks. Later both tried to impress the visitors with their warm hospitality.

While sipping tea Vikas stole a couple of glances at Sanjana and he wasn't surprised to find her doing the same. When they finished tea, the elders got up. Mr. Bhargava and his parents got up to walk around the house. Mrs. Bhargava also stood up and said, "You may like to talk to each other in private." And then she left.

Sanjana lifted her gaze and focused it at him. For a moment he got nervous but then the week's experience of talking with girls stood him in a good stead and he regained composure. Looking in her beautiful eyes, he asked, "Would you like to know anything about me before making up your mind?"

She moved closer to him and asked how many girls he had seen before. He narrated the previous experiences and they had a good hearty laugh. During their talks she opened up and shared her thoughts, her hopes for the marriage. It was a coincidence that they had a lot in common. Half-hour later they became friends. And when their parents entered the room they found them laughing. His father gave a little cough to attract their attention. Both then became serious. The elders were elated when Vikas and Sanjana told them about their decision. In the din of laughter they congratulated and offered sweets to one another.

Vikas got to eat his favorite sweet again. They had hardly settled in when another girl wearing the sari of the same color and design walked in and sat beside him. Nudging Sanjana, she said, "Thank you, Ranjana. You can go now. Your job is over. I'm Sanjana and Vikas has come to see me."

Flabbergasted by the sudden twist of events, he stood up in disbelief. He heard the new girl say, "Vikas, please sit. I'm Sanjana and this is Ranjana, my twin. The marriage proposal is for me. She was playing a prank."

He was too stunned to react. Sometimes he looked at the first girl and sometimes at the second girl unable to know who was who. The elders were busy talking among themselves. Seeing the commotion Mrs. Bhargava turned towards them. She burst out laughing and Mr. Bhargava joined her. After him it was the turn of his parents to express shock looking at the twins, identical from head to toe, dressed in the similar looking saris.

Seeing their plight, Mr. Bhargava explained, "Oh, she is Ranjana. I mean the girl sitting on to the right. She is Sanjana's twin, a few minutes younger. She is always up to some mischief."

"We were surprised when they were born. They resembled so much that it was tough to distinguish one from the other,"

Mrs. Bhargava then narrated her experiences of raising them. "Often I mixed up between the two and ended up giving milk to the same child again."

"How did you resolve the problem?" his father asked.

"In morning I put a black mark on the forehead of Ranjana but she was a naughty girl since her childhood. She would wipe it clean, baffling me."

"You would have gone through a tough time in raising them," his mother said, regaining her poise.

"Ji, in the beginning it was annoying but after sometime I found a way out. I monitored their habits closely and then knew who was who. Thereafter, it was fun bringing them up as they couldn't play any further pranks on us."

"You should share the secret with us," his father urged Mrs. Bhargava.

"Ranjana is naughtier but don't think Sanjana is a simple girl. Today she is behaving innocently but on her day she can be as naughty as Ranjana. There's a subtle difference between the two," Mrs. Bhargava clarified and told them the secret.

His mother, who had followed the conversation, said with a mischievous grin, "Vikas make a note because both will give you a hard time in future."

He blushed and turned to gauge the reaction of girls around whom the entire discussion centered. To his surprise he found the sofa empty. Perhaps they had slipped away. After sometime they returned home. His mother was ecstatic. In consultation with family panditji she fixed the marriage date after a month. A day later Vikas returned to his job after finalizing the list of invitees with them.

The week before the wedding day was hectic for him and he wanted it to get over soon so that he could spend time with Sanjana. He married Sanjana in a glittering ceremony.

It was a typical, traditional Hindu marriage marked by confusion, drama and tantrums of some unsatisfied relatives. Most guests had plenty of fun. Two days after marriage they moved out for honeymoon leaving his parents to see off the relatives.

Weeklong honeymoon was short but fun. They got to know each other. Both shared their pasts, planned their present and dreamed about their future. While he wanted to tell her all about himself, she was keen to know about his mother—her likes, her dislikes, etc after learning about her illness. During that period he often found her sad and pensive. He knew she was thinking about his mother. The revelation about mother's imminent death had shaken her from within and she had resolved to spend as much time as possible with her mother-in-law.

A day prior to the departure, she confided in him that she wanted to spend more time with his mother. He agreed hiding his reluctance under a fake smile. And moments later he felt ashamed of himself for thinking about his desires and not his ailing mother. That moment Sanjana proved a better human being than him. He felt proud of her.

For a brief period when they stayed at home they saw little of Ranjana. She had come a few times to his house and spent time with her sister. However, she hadn't forgotten to smile when he saw her. One day he was kissing Sanjana when someone called him and he moved out to meet his childhood friend. After seeing him off, he rushed back to the bedroom. There he found Sanjana standing with her back to the door. Tiptoeing behind her, she begged holding her waist, "Sanjana, let's pick up from where we left."

"No, I can't," he heard her mild protest.

"Sanjana, I can't wait."

Then she turned and burst out laughing. "Oh, I too can't wait."

He found her mocking at him and wondered why she was behaving so weirdly. A few moments ago she was kissing him and now she teased him. He was yet to get over the first shock when he heard someone laughing at the door. And when he turned back he saw Sanjana at the door. Both sisters were dressed alike. It seemed they had planned it together.

Discomfiture was writ large on his face. He apologized to Ranjana for the gaffe. At his cost the sisters had a good laugh and an entertaining evening. Till then he hadn't realized how close the twins were emotionally. While leaving Mumbai he invited Ranjana to come and stay with them. Her smart response was that she would come to his place whether he invited her or not, as she couldn't live without Sanjana for too long.

Alone in Mumbai he almost talked to his mother and Sanjana daily for hours. From their talks he gathered that they had developed a great admiration for each other. It gave him huge satisfaction to learn they clicked well. His wait didn't last long as Sanjana joined him after a fortnight. And in the coming days she handled his passionate restiveness well with her disarming smile. She was the perfect wife one could wish for. He envied his luck to get such a compassionate girl as his soulmate. Both lived a blissful life, expecting no interference from relatives. After all, they hadn't spent a month together alone. But when he got a call from Ranjana that she was coming to Mumbai, he couldn't say no. In fact, Sanjana was glad to get her twin over for sometime.

So, when Ranjana landed up at their place, they gave her a warm welcome. The evenings became livelier with her arrival as she regaled them with her unending stories of her college days. During one narration she got serious and told them she had fallen in love with Sudhanshu, her classmate, and they wanted to marry.

Vikas congratulated her and asked, "Where's the hitch?"

And before he realized, Sanjana spoke, "Sudhanshu is a Brahmin, not of our caste. Papa won't agree to this proposal and she wants you to convince him."

He looked at Ranjana for affirmation. She nodded. He said, "All right, I'll speak to your papa as soon as possible. I'll discuss it with him in person."

After a week she went home. As promised Vikas went to the in-laws' house and discussed the matter with his father-in-law, who didn't budge but in the end he listened to his logic and gave his grudging consent. He met Sudhanshu and found him a smart and likable guy.

After graduation Ranjana got a well-paying job and married Sudhanshu. Vikas went there a week before marriage to oversee the arrangements and help his in-laws. When Ranjana and Sudhanshu went for their honeymoon he returned to Mumbai. Thereafter he got busy in the job and Sanjana in hers, and both forgot to speak with Ranjana. He felt guilty when he received her call after a few months and was surprised she didn't scold him for not phoning her. He assumed she had found a good friend in Sudhanshu and was happy in her married life. In between she came to their house, sometime alone and a few times with her husband, and she looked good except that she had lost her chirpiness. He guessed the marriage sobered people down and she was no different. After all, he had noticed Sanjana lose a bit of liveliness after marriage.

Four years later a storm devastated their lives when one day they heard that Ranjana lay in the hospital battling her life. They took the first flight and reached the hospital. A crestfallen, teary-eyed father-in-law greeted them in the corridor from whom he learned that she had attempted suicide by consuming poison. Narrating the incident the father fell down in the chair. Vikas was too overwhelmed to offer him any comforting words. After a while he recovered and both walked to the ICU where he met an inconsolable mother-in-law sitting by Ranjana's bedside.

He walked to the bed and found Ranjana in deep slumber. The duty nurse told him that she was out of danger, recovering from the shock and he could talk to her once she woke up. A few minutes later he met the doctor who told him that she had escaped a narrow death.

"Doctor, what can we do to make sure she doesn't try it again?" he asked, too terrified to utter the word, suicide.

"Give her a lot of love and care. She is in a terrible marriage," was all he was willing to reveal that moment.

It took him no time to understand the genesis of her problem. He had guessed it all along during the journey. The doctor had confirmed his worst fears but what had surprised him the most was that a brave girl like her had thought of suicide. During four years that he had known her, he had found her a gutsy girl who could weather any storm. That incident had shaken him completely.

While he waited at her bedside many thoughts crossed his mind. He had asked her parents to go home and bring something to eat for everybody. And his joy trickled down through tears when she opened her eyes. Her lips quivered but no words escaped them. Her tears flowed, instead. He said nothing to her and waited for her to get home.

In the house he got the first opportunity to talk to her, alone. It was her wish and no one objected. Without wasting time, he asked, with lump in his throat, "Ranjana, why?"

She couldn't speak for a long time but cried non-stop, her head on his shoulders. He let her drown her sorrows in the streaming tears. And when she was herself, she narrated him her trauma, life with Sudhanshu.

She spoke, he listened. Hers was a blissful marriage gone terribly wrong. What she told him about Sudhanshu was despicable. He wasn't the man he had met. The man beat her, traumatized her and humiliated her daily. Why had she tolerated him for so long? She could give no reason.

He was left speechless when she finished. It baffled him that how could a twenty-first century, educated and career girl suffer unspeakable miseries in her marriage? How could a brave girl like her ever think of suicide? He tried to come to terms with the complexities of her mind and pondered how to begin.

"Ranjana, you broke the promise you gave me," he said.

Her calm, philosophical refrain was, "Perhaps God saved me to seek your forgiveness. What could I do? You weren't there to help me. Ever girl isn't as lucky as Sanjana."

"Ranjana, I'm not as good as you think."

"You are the man a normal girl can aspire for," she shot back.

Before she could praise me further, I tried to reason with her, "Ranjana, life is too precious to be wasted for any person. You are a brave girl. I'm sure you will get over this soon and find a better man in future."

Looking at the ceiling, she asked, "Do you believe in rebirth?"

The strange question shook him from within, but he retained his poise. He said, "Yeah."

"Then promise me one thing. In the next birth you will be mine, mine alone," she said. A faint smile of hope had returned on her face.

"What about Sanjana?" he said.

"Don't worry about her. We don't be born as twins. Moreover, she has you now. It's my turn in the next birth," her voice had gained some strength.

He knew there was no way out of this dilemma. His answer was crucial for her future, for her survival perhaps. It didn't take him long to decide. He moved closer to her and whispered, "Yeah, Ranjana. I will be yours, all yours in the next birth. Now promise, you won't repeat this stupid thing ever."

"I won't," she grinned. Her innocent smile assured him she was on path to recovery.

Minutes later they came out of the room. She was completely changed, bringing a smile on ever face. Sanjana wondered what her husband had done to cheer up her traumatized sister. That night in the bedroom she asked him with a mischievous grin, "Viki, what did you tell Ranjana? She's much better now."

He said seriously, "That's a secret between us. Would you like to hear it?"

"No, better it remains a secret otherwise it will lose its effect. Perhaps you don't know how much I love her. I can sacrifice anything to see her alive and happy."

He had no doubt she loved her twin but he wondered why she didn't insist him to reveal the secret to her.

A Night in Ajanta

"So, where's my hubby taking me to this winter?"

"Caves."

"At twenty-five, I've no intention of doing the penance in the Himalayas," she winked.

"Neither do I," he said, with a mischievous half-grin. "I meant the Ajanta and Ellora Caves in Maharashtra."

"I guess that's a fascinating idea," she smiled. "Will it be an adventure or a pleasure trip?"

"I guess a bit of the both."

"Which one will be more, adventure or pleasure?" she quizzed, rolling her naughty eyes.

"Depends. Which one you want more?" he was at his wittiest best.

"Well, leave that to me," she said, rising. "You plan the trip. I'll go and prepare something to eat. We are late for dinner."

He watched her leave the bedroom. They—Mohit and Shalakha—were in the fifth year of marriage. Theirs had been a happy life, full of love, care and compassion. Like any other couple, they also had disagreements and squabbles, but those had been too few to affect their relationship. As a sensible couple, they respected the need for space and hence didn't encroach into each other's privacy. Without fail, they went for yearly vacations during which they discovered new and surprising aspects of their personalities in addition to discovering the place. And during those holidays they found a thousand reasons to love each other. As time grew, so did their love. Thus the vacations became inseparable parts of their lives and they never missed them despite their hectic work schedule.

Both worked in different companies and slogged round the clock, eighteen hours a day, six days a week, and often forewent regular meals, sleep and sex. Only the brave people survived in the tough and ruthless corporate world that broke a couple of marriages every month.

In the yearlong courtship and the following years after the marriage, they had shared their failed love affairs and their uncertain presents. They didn't hide anything from each other. The simple logic was that they never wanted any skeletons to tumble out of the cupboards later and rock their marriage. Therefore, they built their relationship on mutual trust and transparency. And they shared with each other their dreams, however stupid and insignificant those were. Like several couples, they too had their ups and downs.

"Mohit, come dinner is ready," her voice cut his thoughts short. He stood up and rushed to the dining table, where she waited for him having laid out the plates and dishes. They had a quiet dinner, sharing many smiles. He gave her generous compliments about the delicious food. Then they went to bed.

A week later they boarded the Devagiri Express for Aurangabad, the city closest to the caves, where they planned to stay for a few days. The journey lasted about seven hours. They reached the railway station at 5 a.m. and checked into the hotel straightway. After some rest, they had breakfast and moved out for the Ajanta Caves.

Vinayak Salunkhe, the taxi driver was a talkative person who spoke fluent Hindi and English. During the two-hour journey, he told them a few fascinating folktales about the place. At 10 a.m. they reached Ajanta, on the downslope of a hill section. The place was sparkling clean and had well-maintained lawns. On the raised ground were the cottages run by the state tourism department. In the center, two rows of shops sold almost everything from the stones to embroidered bags to several other items that one found at any tourist place.

Pointing at the tea stall Shalakha told him that she wanted to have hot tea before moving further to the Ajanta Caves. He couldn't say no and they halted at the shop. Many shopkeepers gave them an eager look as they had tea. And once they finished, a dozen sellers surrounded them and urged them to buy their items. A couple of them gifted her some cheap stones to lure her.

When he saw her show a keen interest in those items, he gave her a gentle nudge, hiding irritation, "Shalu, let's move. You can shop later."

With reluctance she agreed and they moved towards the waiting buses, which ferried the tourists to the cave site, about four kilometers from there. They boarded the bus and moved on. After about ten minutes they got down from the bus. He bought the tickets, hired the guide and then they climbed up the stairs towards the main cave site. The guide narrated them the incident how a British hunter by accident had discovered those caves in 1819 A.D. while on a hunting mission in the jungles there.

The guide stopped at the Cave No 1 and said, "Sir, these are the Buddhist rock-hewn Ajanta caves, horseshoe in shape and rise over the ravine to a steep height of about 250 feet. These cave temples were carved out of the rocks and took about eight hundred years to complete. The oldest cave was created in the second century B.C. and work on these rock caves continued till the sixth century A.D."

"Oh God! It's so amazing," she exclaimed.

"Indeed. It's mind-boggling," he added.

The guide waited for them to digest the enormity and magnificence of the caves. Then he resumed, "Sir, these rock temples depict the grandeur of the ancient Indian sculpture. And the painting, the third art form is added to the cave architecture. It has made Ajanta a world-famous city. These rock paintings aren't found in any other caves in India."

Thereafter, he took them to all the caves and showed them the sculptures and motifs on the walls. Most paintings, destroyed by two thousand years of neglect, had still retained some of their brilliance and evoked instant awe and admiration among the visitors.

"These are lyrics in the stone," she said, her eyes glued to the caves.

Mohit was bewildered by the vivacity of female figures, which had well-curved forms, elongated eyes, attractive mien and ample adornment.

Seeing him stare at the women in the painting, she teased, "Don't get too involved in them. They won't come out of the walls for you."

Embarrassed, he said avoiding eye contact with her, "No, no. I wonder what colours were used on these paintings, which have survived for thousands of years."1

"Liar," she mumbled.

"Did you say anything?" he asked, looking at her.

"Nothing. Let's move ahead," she said.

"OK."

And they followed the guide like tenth-grade students, inquisitive and impatient to learn everything about the cave temples at one go. The guide took them around each cave where they had to remove the shoes and weren't permitted to take pictures inside the caves, lest the flash damaged whatever little was left of those paintings. He told them that there were about thirty caves, some of which were unfinished and negligible. Sixteen of them contained the mural paintings and sculptures. The numbering of the caves was in the consecutive order and had no relation to their chronological sequence of building.

"Is the present entrance the original one?" Shalakha asked.

"No, Ma'am. It doesn't seem so," the guide hesitated. "Entrance to these caves was through the river from where the steps led to the different caves."

"How could the ancient painters make such beautiful paintings?" Mohit asked.

The guide looked at him for a moment and then replied, "The painters in the olden times applied a different technique. First, a rough plaster of clay, cow-dung and rice-husks were laid upon the selected rock surface and a thorough press was given to it. It made a layer about one and a half centimeter in thickness. On this a coat of fine lime was spread to get a smooth surface. The outlines were drawn with the brush and then the colour was applied. The pigment used was of simple materials such as the yellow earth, red ocher, green rock crushed into burnt dust brick, lamp black and copper oxide. After that the second coat was applied. Other brushes were used to fill the colours until the picture bloomed. In the end, the plastic relief was attained by shading with darker lines and toning down the highlights."

"Fascinating," both spoke in unison, marvelling at the guide's knowledge.

"What was the inspiration behind these paintings?" Mohit asked.

The guide felt pricey and spoke with a slight shrug, "The central theme on the wall paintings comes under two heads. One contains the narrative scenes from the Buddha's life and two, the illustrations of the Jataka fables. And within this framework of spirituality an entire pageant of the contemporary life in those times was vividly painted. The walls had the paintings of the Buddha and the Bodhisattvas, and a range of human emotions. The flying *gandharvas* and *apsaras* are fascinating to watch."

"But the paintings on the ceiling are different from those on the walls," she interrupted him.

"Yes Ma'am. Your observation is right. They include geometric designs, floral and ornamental motifs, flying figures of celestial beings, animals, birds and plants."

From there they moved ahead, seeing the viharas, numerous sculptures and listened to a few Jataka tales, which the guide narrated them. Their journey along the caves was mesmerizing and transported them into a different world. Both were awestruck. Once they reached the Cave No 20, they thanked the guide and paid him. He walked back leaving the couple to enjoy a few moments of privacy and solitude.

Bewildered, they looked at the caves for a long time. They said nothing but gazed at the sculptures and murals, and once in a while, exchanged admiring glances. Lost in thoughts, they lost the track of time. It jolted them when the security guard came to them and said, "Sahib, time is over. Everyone has moved back. You are the last couple. It's about to get dark. Please rush back; otherwise, you will miss the last bus."

The guard returned after warning them.

"Oh no. We didn't realize it was getting dark," he said.

"What if we don't get the bus?" she asked, worry lines appearing on her face.

"We can do nothing. I guess we'll have to walk back then."

"All right," she pulled his arm and they rushed back, climbing up and down a series of stairs till they reached the entrance.

The parking looked deserted. A man told them that the last bus had left about fifteen minutes back.

"What!" she yelled in disgust.

The man suggested, "You can stay for the night in the hotel here."

"Thanks," Mohit said and looked at her for approval. She was worried. He knew she would be in no mood to stay in that desolate place.

He asked the man, "How much time will it take to walk back to the main area?"

"Less than a half-hour."

"Thank you."

They started walking, hand in hand. It was getting dark. He switched on the torch to see the road alignment.

"We should have stayed in the hotel here," she said.

"No, the better option would be to spend the night in one of those caves," he squeezed her hand.

"I know what's on your mind."

"What?"

"You want to live your fantasy with me, but I'm not one of the women you were ogling," she teased.

He blushed. They strolled back and after a half-hour reached the cottages, most of which were vacant. The manager gave them one cottage and the waiter brought them hot tea. Sitting in the veranda, they sipped tea and gazed at the horizon. In the fast fading light nothing was visible except the hills' silhouettes.

"Good, we decided to stay for the night here. There was no point in going back to Aurangabad at this late hour," she said, between the sips.

"Yeah. We'll celebrate this night in a special way," he winked.

She pretended not to hear him and said, "Isn't this place so wonderful, so calm."

"Absolutely," he couldn't say anything further as the waiter had returned.

The boy showed them the menu. They settled for the vegetarian food and after freshening up had dinner. Thereafter, they walked around the place for some time, enjoying the mild chill. The place was totally deserted when the staff went to sleep.

"Shalu, you look so beautiful," he whispered, pressing her hand.

"I suppose not as beautiful as those women in the cave paintings that held your prolonged gaze and admiration," she spoke in half jest, half jealousy.

"Shalu, I'm not joking. I mean it," he became serious.

"Sorry Mohit. I believe you," she said. "I hope you want to spend the night walking in the dark. A while ago you said about celebrating something."

"Of course."

In the streetlight falling on his face, she saw his mischievous grin. Without wasting time, they rushed back to the room. In seconds they were in each other's arms, cuddling, kissing, patting and discovering the pleasure of togetherness. And both ensured that was an exceptional, long night, unlike the routine ones they had at home.

In the morning the waiter woke them up with hot tea. In the veranda sipping tea, she asked, "Mohit, in the sleep you were murmuring Pragya, Pragya. Who's this Pragya?"

"Oh," he smiled. "It was a dream."

"A romantic one, I suppose," she asked.

"Yeah. Would you like to listen to it?"

"Of course," she said, fidgeting on the chair.

"Won't you feel jealous," a naughty grin played on his lips.

"Sure, I'll. But I can handle a bit of jealousy caused by a harmless Pragya," she forced a smile.

"All right," he looked at the distant hills to draw inspiration and then began:

"Last night I had an unusual dream. It was about 400 A.D., I guess. I don't recollect the exact year. The Buddhist King ruling this region decided to resume excavation of the cave temples for the Buddhist monks at Ajanta. The place already had half a dozen caves that had been excavated earlier. Soon the entire place was flooded with people—the architects, the sculptors, the artisans, the rock cutters, the diggers, the masons, the painters and the labourers. I was a painter and my name was Ugantara. Like other painters, the king's men summoned me too and so I reached this place from my native village, about fifty miles east of Ajanta.

It was an incredible sight, buzzing with activities. The Waghora River flowing through the two adjoining hill ranges provided the water for all of us. The existing caves gave us valuable information to resume the excavation further. The oldest cave had been made six hundred years ago.

We resumed the work but everybody knew that it would take generations to complete. I was surprised that before us many generations had worked in those caves. We worked under the supervision of Chakrapani, the famous painter of that era. He was a genius and for the amateur painters like us it was an awesome experience. The Buddhist monks supervised our work. Most paintings were related to the Buddha and the Bodhisattvas, and illustrations from the Jataka tales. One day when I was painting a beautiful woman, a sweet voice from behind interrupted me, "The nose is a bit too long."

Surprised, I turned back to see who was trying to teach me how to paint. A foot away stood a gorgeous woman, giving my painting a critical look. I tried to avoid her but she spoke again, "Don't you think the woman's nose in that painting is a bit too long and not in the center of her face."

Stung by her criticism, I had a closer look at my painting. She was right in her observation. The nose indeed was long and not in the center. I nodded and acknowledged her concern. She asked me to have a close look at her nose to get the proper perspective for the painting. I watched her face and corrected my mistake in the painting.

During the break, she introduced me. Her name was Pragyavati. We talked for some time and then she left. Thereafter, we met daily during the break. After a few days she brought me home-cooked food as a routine. Often I skipped my work and met her in the nearby forest where we ate lunch together. I fell in love with her and wasn't able to concentrate. My work suffered. Other painters noticed the sudden change in me.

A week later she confessed her love to me. Our secret meetings in the forest went on uninterrupted. I had to make excuses to get away from the work. My friends suspected that I was involved with a woman, but they didn't object. In fact, they had to make impromptu excuses for my absence when the guards asked them about me.

One day I suggested to her that we elope, get married and start our lives in a new place, far away from there.

Her response was deliberate and patient. She said, "No, Ugantara. I don't think it's a good idea. You can't leave your work unfinished. We should wait for it to get completed. You are doing something that would be remembered for centuries long after we are gone from this world."

That moment I felt childish and foolish. She was calm and had displayed better sense of purpose. She was conscious of the immense importance of the work going on in those caves. After her counselling I resumed my work with full gusto. And despite my hectic schedule we met regularly and our relationship blossomed for about a year. A friend of my mine, who perhaps had spied on me, learned about my love affair. He accepted my fondness for Pragya but expressed concern about our future because he knew something that I didn't until he told me one day.

Taking me aside, he whispered, "Ugantara, you are in love with a woman who isn't your destiny."

"Why?" I said, getting anxious.

"Steel yourself. What I'm going to tell you now, isn't good news at all."

"Go ahead, I'm listening," I said.

"Pragya isn't a commoner. She is a princess. Confirmed news from inside the palace is that she is getting married to a prince within a few months. So, my advice to you is to forget her and carry on with your life."

My heart began to sink after listening to him. I knew what he said could be true but somehow I wasn't ready to accept it. So, I asked Pragya the next day. The question brought sadness on her face. With misty eyes she told me that she was getting married to the prince at the insistence of her parents. She was not in a state to refuse them. Her father had a small kingdom. The powerful king wanted Pragya as a bride for his son. Her refusal could result in the war, which her father was sure to lose. That could mean untold miseries for the people of her father's kingdom. And she wasn't a selfish princess who would sacrifice the poor folks' lives for the sake of her love.

Therefore, she consented to marry the man whom she hadn't seen or met until then. A steady stream of tears rolled down her eyes as she narrated her helplessness. She felt guilty of abandoning me. I consoled her and said that I had no hard feelings for her and she was free to marry the prince as per the dictates of her father.

Before parting on a happy note, we promised each other to reunite in the future birth. With a lump in my throat, I watched her walk out of my life forever. That moment is still etched on my mind. It fills my heart with a sharp pain when I think of it. Later I returned to complete my unfinished works. Thereafter, I painted her in every woman. In fact, all my paintings carry her reflections in some form or the other.

After her exit from my life I lost interest in everything. And when I got the news of her marriage, I lost whatever little hope I had in life. I became irregular in my meals, rest and sleep and fell ill. Seeing my pitiable condition, Chakrapani relieved me and asked me to go home.

A year after her marriage I returned home and fell ill. On the insistence of my parents, I showed myself to the local *vaidya*, whose medicines failed to cure me. I never married and carried her memories in my heart as long as I lived. Fortunately, I didn't live long to suffer her separation and died within a year of coming home."

Mohit finished the dream and wiped his teary eyes. She held him in a tight embrace. After a while, he stopped crying and separated from her. She got up and poured tea in their glasses.

"How was she to look at?" she asked in a serious tone.

Suddenly his sadness vanished and a smile returned on his face. Peeping in her eyes, he said, “She was a dark-eyed, beautiful woman.”

“I mean what were her features like,” she probed further, suppressing a tinge of jealousy, which had crept in her heart.

“You mean the broad hips and big bosom,” he said seriously. “She was an ancient beauty with heavy features.”

For a second Shalakha’s gaze fell on her chest and hips. A deep sense of inadequacy filled her heart. Tempted to know more about his dream woman, she probed further, “What was her face like?”

“Oh, Shalu. You won’t believe what I’m going to tell you,” he whispered, coming closer to her. “Her face was exactly like yours.”

“Come on, Mohit. Give me a break.”

“Shalu,” he said, giving her an intent look, “Don’t you believe me?”

“It’s a flattering dream. I’m ready to believe it,” she mumbled and hugged him. She didn’t want to know the complete truth of his dream.

Sailor's Wife

Tucked inside a five-kilo quilt, Ashutosh Sinha was in deep slumber. He was at home on a weeklong holiday. Though Varanasi during December was chilly, the city was warm during the day, unlike Shimla where he worked as a manager in a holiday resort. It was his second night at home. In the midst of a fascinating dream, he felt someone pull the quilt from over his head.

"Mummy, let me sleep. Why are you waking me? It's still dark," he begged and protested, seeing his mother at the bedside.

"Ashu *beta*, it's 9 o'clock and the sun is up. Why don't you go to the *sutti* (the wholesale vegetable market) and get me some fresh vegetables from there?" she urged him.

"Come on, Mummy. I haven't come home to fetch you vegetables from the *sutti*," his mild protest continued. "Why don't you buy it from the vendor who comes daily in our colony?"

"I often buy it from him but he fleeces me because he knows I can't go to the *sutti*. I used to go there with your papa. Things are so cheap and fresh there," she looked at him.

He sprang out of the bed and said, "All right, Mummy. I'll go. Give me a jute bag and the list."

"Wait a minute. Have tea and don't forget to put on your jacket. It's cold outside," she said, handing him a cup of hot tea.

He took the cup with a smile. So, she knew he wouldn't refuse her and had planned everything in advance, he thought between the sips. When he looked at her jaded face his heart went out to her. His mother was a lecturer in the college and lived alone. His father had left her when he was a child, too young to understand the meaning of the word 'divorce'. As a kid when he had cried for his father, she had fabricated lame excuses to pacify him.

It wasn't until twelve when she told him the truth that his father wouldn't live with them anymore. A few family friends told him that his father had left his mother for a younger woman. That was about ten years ago. Till date he couldn't figure out why his father had dumped such a caring and beautiful woman. He had heard rumours that the woman with whom his father lived wasn't half as beautiful as his mother, who looked many years younger than her age. Her face still carried the youthful charm and childhood innocence, though loneliness had taken some of the sheen off her beauty.

Post divorce his mother had maintained the dignity and grace for which she was known and respected among their relatives. She had never let him feel his father's absence as she had given him so much love and care. After learning his father's character he had no desire to see him. Neither had he felt hatred nor any anxiety for him. In fact, he harboured no feelings, good or bad, for his father. Only a fool could leave such a loving and caring woman like his mother, he was convinced. His father had lost more than his mother after their break up.

In a hurry he gulped down the last cold sip and rushed down the stairs with the bag. The *sutti* was about a furlong, walking distance, from home. And within a half-hour he was at the market entrance. The area was flooded with people of all faiths and genders. Majority of the buyers were the retailers and vendors. The old folks, perhaps pestered by their sons and daughters-in-law, were out in that chilly morning to buy vegetables while the young people had chosen to stay within the warm confines of the house.

The place gave an amusing spectacle. It was chaotic and dusty with sellers shouting at the top of their voices, some of which had gone hoarse, to attract buyers to them. The cows, goats and buffaloes roamed the area, eating vegetables here and there. And when a seller got involved in haggling with the buyers, the cattle made away with a generous helping of vegetables and by the time the owner realized it was too late. The poor cattle received thrashing and abuses for their daylight, daring theft but they didn't seem to mind the beating at all because they moved away to another pile to pick up more vegetables.

Piles of fresh vegetables lay around everywhere; some under the concrete shed, some under the polythene leans-to and others under the open sky. As far as his eyes went he saw the vegetables and more vegetables. Tomatoes, potatoes, brinjals, onions, ladyfingers, cucumbers, cauliflowers, capsicums, garlic, chilies, spinach and gourd were piled up all around the place. At every heap the buyers haggled with the sellers. After making a successful deal the vendors were carting their purchase away in the pull carts as they were in a hurry to sell it on the streets and in the colonies.

For a few moments he stood there amused at the chaotic scene and then went to a lone corner to pick up the vegetables. He coughed to draw the seller's attention to him, took out his list and started reading, "Arey, *bhaiya*, give me one kilo tomatoes, one potato............"

His reading was cut short by the giggles that came from close by. Curious, he turned and found a woman laughing under the scarf wrapped around her face. The seller joined her. Peeved, he looked at her, at the seller and then asked her, "Arey, what happened? Why are you laughing at me?"

She removed her scarf, showing her pretty face and then spoke, "It seems you are new to this place?"

"Yeah."

"That's why you are asking the vegetables in half-kilos and kilos. People don't come here to buy them in small quantities. Nobody buys less than half a *paseri.*"

It further confused him. Looking at her, he asked, "What's a *paseri*?"

Her prompt reply was, "Almost equal to five kilos."

Minutes later she helped him in choosing the right variety of vegetables by smelling them, feeling them between her tender fingers and even tasting a few. He looked perplexed and impressed by her knowledge. For her it was an elaborate ritual, he noticed and hence didn't disturb her.

"Don't forget to get free coriander and chilies from the seller," she said, with a glint in her eyes. "Nothing gives a woman greater satisfaction in the market than these freebies."

He gave her an admiring look.

Once she had finished she turned to him and found him shivering.

"It seems this weather isn't suiting you. Why don't we have hot tea?" she suggested.

"Yeah, that's a good idea."

And they walked towards the tea stall, under a shanty plastic lean-to in one corner of the *sutti*. She asked for two cups of tea, which the shopkeeper served them instantly.

Sipping hot tea, he asked, "Are you regular to this place?"

"Yeah."

"Oh, I'm so stupid I haven't asked your name yet, though we have been together for the last half-hour," he said.

"I'm Vaishali," was her prompt response.

"I'm Ashutosh."

With formal introduction over he felt free with her having shed his initial inhibitions. "In which college do you study?" he asked.

"Come on. Do I look that young? I'm married. I did my graduation a couple of years back," she smiled. The morning chill had made her cheeks rosy, the blush deepened their colour.

"It seems your hubby is sleeping and he has sent you to buy the vegetables in this cold weather," he teased.

"No, no. It's not so. In fact, I live with my parents. My husband's in South Africa," she said with a mild protest.

"What is he doing there?"

"He is in the Merchant Navy. Last month his ship sailed for South Africa."

"So, you are a sailor's wife."

"No, he not a sailor but an officer," she objected.

"Ma'am, perhaps you don't know that all men on the ship irrespective of their status are called the sailors," he explained.

"Sorry, I didn't know that. Perhaps I've a lot to learn from you," she said, rolling her eyes.

For a moment he was flabbergasted, trying to understand the hidden intent behind her words. And then it occurred to him that she could be a great company in the town where he had no friends. Regaining poise, he shot back, "I too need to learn many things from you."

"Like?" she acted surprised.

"How to choose the vegetables and haggle with the sellers," he conjured a lie.

"It's just that or something else," she muttered.

It was his turn to be surprised. She gave enough hints to him to make the necessary moves. He stole a glance at her and found her lost in thoughts. "Let's move," he said, drawing her attention.

"Yeah, how was the tea?" she asked.

"It's strong and hot," he said in pensive mood.

She smiled.

"When do you come here to buy vegetables?" he asked.

"Oh, I see. You want to know on which days you can find me here," she winked.

He reddened. She didn't wish to add to his discomfiture and so replied, "I come here on Wednesdays and Saturdays. I hope this satisfies your curiosity."

"Two more days before we meet again," he murmured.

"What are you thinking about?" she asked.

"Nothing."

He seemed too eager to meet her. She was also drawn to him. While his impatience was written on his face, she hid hers behind her face. The women were skilled in the art of concealing their true feelings. And she was no different.

"Well, we will meet on next Wednesday," she said, extending her hand.

"Do you read minds?" he asked, shaking hand.

"Yeah, sometimes," she gave a mischievous grin. "But don't ask me what's going on in your mind at this moment."

After a while she went home after exchanging a warm good-bye with him. He watched her go until she vanished in the crowd. At home mother greeted with hot tea and questioning glances. Though she didn't ask him anything, he could guess the cause of her concern. He had spent a long time in the market.

After breakfast his mother got busy in the routine household chores while he watched TV, shuffling through the newspapers. In between he thought of the sailor's wife. He tried to recollect her name but couldn't despite straining his mind. Then he abandoned his efforts and instead preferred to remember her as the sailor's wife. To him it sounded romantic, mystical.

Her behavior that Saturday morning had baffled him and he mulled over it for next couple of days. Then he decided to go on next Wednesday to meet her, to know more about her. Wrapped in a shawl, she looked attractive and affable. He found no harm in meeting her again.

He woke up at daybreak, shaved, had a quick shower, wore fresh clothes and put on nice smelling cologne. His mother was surprised to see him up in the morning.

With a grin, she asked, "Ashu, strange? Are you going out somewhere today?"

"No, Mummy. I thought you might need the vegetables, so I got ready," he lied.

"Oh, I never knew my son is so concerned about me, or it's something else. I don't recall any good looking girl coming to the *sutti* to buy vegetables," she teased him.

"No, Mummy. It's not that," he was defensive. "As long as I'm here I would like to help you out."

"All right, I believe you. Wait a second, I'll make the list."

After a while he was on the way to the *sutti* with a jute bag in hand. With spring in his steps, song on his lips and hope in his heart, he moved on. After spending some time in her search, he spotted her haggling with a seller. Standing before a huge pile she was buying tomatoes.

Though he wished to meet her soon, he wanted it to look like a chance meeting. He didn't want to give her an impression that he was dying to see her. So, he also roamed for some time and pretended to bargain with a few sellers loud enough to draw her attention. With steady steps he moved in her direction. And when he was haggling like a novice at the neighboring shop, she heard him or pretended to hear him. She saw him and said, "What are you buying today?"

"Oh, good you have come. Now I can breathe easy," his surprise was mechanical and noticeable.

"Why?"

"I need your help in buying the vegetables," he said.

"OK, then let's go."

They finished their purchases within an hour and then settled for hot tea at the same teashop. This time, though, the tea break was a little longer and quieter unlike the last time. Both were pensive and anxious. Once tea was over he broke the silence, "Vaishali, don't you think we need to meet in a nice and better place?"

"You mean in some restaurant or coffee house."

"Yeah."

"What for?"

Caught in her web of words he was unsettled for a few moments. Then he regained his composure and said, "Perhaps for coffee."

"coffee?"

"Yeah, coffee."

Both knew they were lying, but lived in the false notion that neither knew about it.

"What are you thinking about?" she asked, in an anxious tone.

"Where should we go for the coffee?"

"With jute bags in our hands," her white teeth glistened when she laughed aloud.

"Of course, not. We can meet in the evening, but I don't know any decent place. Can you suggest one?"

"I was joking. All right, we'll meet in the Delight Coffee House," she said and then explained him how to reach there.

With hopes in their hearts they parted. During breakfast, he asked his mother, "Mummy, are you going out somewhere in the evening?"

"No, why?"

"I want to go for a long drive."

"Date," was her inquisitive query.

"Come on, Mummy. You know I know no one here. All my college mates have moved out. It's just a long drive," he evaded.

"OK, but be careful and don't venture too far on the secluded road that goes to Chunar," she cautioned.

"Mummy, don't worry. Nobody is going to kidnap me. We have no fat bank balance, or property," he said.

"You live in a peaceful city and hence don't know how bad this place has become in the last few decades. They can kidnap anyone even for petty ransom."

"OK, Mummy, I'll be careful," he cut her short to avoid her stories about kidnappings that had taken place in the past one year.

Their conversation finished, as did their breakfast. And they got busy with their activities. While his mother moved out to the college, he stayed at home to go through the grind of another dull day. Except for reading books, magazines and newspapers he had nothing else to do. Six-hour compulsory load shedding during the day made it difficult to either watch TV or work on the computer. And he didn't like going out for movies alone.

He waited and made plans. As the evening approached he got ready to leave. After a long shower he put on a light blue shirt, a pair of jeans and wore his favorite perfume. Stuffing some notes in the wallet, he ran down the stairs. Moments later he was headed towards the coffee house. Though never a stickler for time, he didn't want to be late for that date and miss her, the sailor's mystical wife.

And to his utter surprise he found her waiting inside the coffee house. "Sorry, I got delayed," he offered her instant apology, sitting down.

"No, you aren't late. I'm early," she said putting him at ease. "So, what would you've?"

"A hot coffee."

"Anything to eat?"

"No, I had late lunch. You can order for yourself."

"I don't feel like eating anything."

"Yeah, I can understand that. You are conscious about your figure."

Her cheeks became pink. She gestured to the waiter. After placing order for two coffees, her gaze returned to him. He was stealing glances at her.

"Is there anything wrong with my dress," she got nervous.

"No, I was admiring you dress."

"So, you are afraid of telling a married woman that she looks beautiful," she teased. "You can be more generous. At this moment my husband is thousands of miles away to cause you any harm."

He laughed and then whispered, “You look so gorgeous in this dress.”

She felt the gush of his warm breath touch her bosom. She shot back, “Perhaps, prettier than what I look in the *sutti* buying vegetables.”

“You look attractive any time of the day, in any dress,” he was effusive in his praise.

“Ashutosh, you are a magician,” she said and then lapsed in a trance. “It has been ages since someone told me I’m beautiful. My parents have no time to praise me for anything. They consider me a burden and want to palm me off to my husband as soon as possible.”

“Oh, I’m sorry if I caused you any distress.”

“No, you didn’t. The man who did isn’t bothered whether I’m dead or alive.”

“Who?”

“My husband. He has sailed to a far off place and doesn’t bother to give me regular calls. His last call was a month ago. He spoke from South Africa. I don’t know where he is today.”

“Don’t worry, he might be caught up is some important work. He’ll call you soon,” he tried to mollify her.

She became quiet and they had their coffee in silence. Except for a few people the place was empty and gave them enough privacy to talk to one another in free and frank manner.

Once she finished coffee, she asked him, “Are you married?”

“No.”

“Perhaps that’s the reason you don’t understand the worries of a lonely wife,” her voice was sad. “I’m a human too and sometimes I do fall sick, and that’s when I need someone to take me to the doctor, someone to care for me. But for the last year and half I had no one to ask me how I was. I would have fallen sick a dozen times and except for once; I went to the doctor alone."

"Why?" he expressed surprise.

"My parents were too busy to take me to the doctor. Every time I went to a different doctor. Do you know, why?"

"No," he nodded.

"I was fearful the same doctor might try to develop familiarity with me and take advantage of an unaccompanied woman. Every day I read about the doctors doing horrifying things with their helpless patients. I also became fearful each time I went to see the doctor," tears streamed down as she spoke.

"Vaishali, please don't cry," he bent forward to wipe her tears but she stopped him. He offered, "You can come with me. A long drive would give you some comfort."

She nodded, wiping her eyes. After a while they moved out of the coffee house and within minutes they were out of the hullabaloo of the city, moving on a secluded road. During an hour's drive they shared a few glances and several silences before he stopped the car near a hillock. For miles they hadn't come across any human being; motorist, pedestrian, or villager. He opened the car for her and then they moved towards a forlorn rock, at the base of the hill.

He helped her sit down and then asked, "Why don't you write to your husband and ask him to take you where he stays?"

With a puzzled look she replied, "He can't take me with him because he doesn't stay in India for more than a few weeks. After marriage he had taken me to his parent's home, but once they expired about a year back, I've no place to go except to live with my parents."

"Why? He can always hire an apartment in a good city where you can stay and take up a job to occupy yourself," he argued.

"Yeah, that's an alternative I suggested to him when he dumped me here after his parents expired but he declined."

"Why? What were his reasons?"

"He couldn't leave me at an unknown place for the fear of my safety and when I told him to hire a house here, my parents objected. So, willy-nilly I landed up staying with them," she paused. "In the beginning my parents were supportive of my problems but as the months passed by their behavior changed towards me. They couldn't tolerate the jibes of neighbours and relatives who had started spreading canards against me."

"Like."

"My husband has left me because I'm barren, or I've left him because he is impotent, or he is already married, or he has found out about my earlier love affair and hence divorced me. My parents have to listen to all this and perhaps much more. And when they hear something like this they take it out on me. In fact, they give me the ultimatum to call my husband and go with him forever. I would have jumped in the Ganges by now had it not been for the tacit support of my mother, but even her patience is wearing thin, of late."

"Oh, I'm so sorry," he spoke, looking at the continuous flow of her tears. He was tempted to move over to her, take her in his arms and wipe her tears. But something held him from doing that. Perhaps his strict upbringing that considered touching a married woman a sin; leave offering her any emotional comfort. For a while he debated in his mind, fought with his conscious and then stood up, having made up his mind.

He took her in his strong arms and murmured, "Vaishali, please don't cry anymore." He wiped her tears and whispered,

"Smile makes you more attractive. Did you ever notice that dimples appear when you grin?"

Her cries subsided with every passing moment. She melted in his arms and rested her head on his chest. In her lonesome hours she, in a man's hug, looked so pretty and so vulnerable. For a while both lay quiet, feeling their heavy breathing and hearts pounding. Then he looked at her face in admiration. Her soft, sensuous touch sent a shiver down his spine. He went weak at the knees and tried hard to control his desire to kiss her waiting wet lips. The temptation consumed him and before he could think anything rational, his lips were on hers in a passionate lock. Her lips quivered and responded. Then the heat of the passion took them in its arms.

In those heady and fleeting moments, he said several times, "Vaishali, I love you, I love you…….."

The music of those words descended deeper and deeper into her heart. It sent her into another world. With every second, his grip tightened and kiss deepened. A year's pent-up emotions and passion inside a woman's body began to unleash. It was the most exquisite experience; she had in married life. Ashutosh was a caring, patient and wise lover. He knew how to make a woman make feel special and different. Therefore, she wanted to savour each moment for posterity, for she didn't know whether she would ever get those moments again in life.

After a while they lay exhausted in each other's arms. In the deepening darkness of the night, a nascent calm stretched for miles. In that ocean of stillness their minds were anxious, their hearts restless. They knew they belonged to each other in body and soul, but a doubt lingered about the future. In the midst of tranquility and turbulence those moments of togetherness seemed to last until eternity. Then the sudden sounds in the distance broke their trance and embrace. They got worried, put on their clothes and gave each other a quick, warm hug. With smiles on their faces they separated. That evening's experience gave him the courage to take his life's most important decision.

That moment he decided to marry her.

Unmindful of the surroundings and bizarre locale, he said, "Vaishali, I love you. Will you marry me?"

For a second she fell silent. The proposal struck her like a thunderbolt. She withdrew into her gloomy existence. It was the sunray with which she wanted to light up her world, but she was scared of the shadows of doubts that threatened to

extinguish that ray. Despite misgivings, she thought of taking a chance and said, "I need time to think."

"All right," his heart jumped in joy.

Minutes later they hurried back home and wanted to reach there before their parents got worried. En route he, like a teenager in love, praised her. She responded with cute smiles. When he was about to enter the city, he halted and said again, "Vaishali, I want to marry you."

Shocked by his admission of love than the question of marriage, she pondered. It was tough for her to answer him that moment. She didn't want to lose him, but at the same time she didn't wish to do anything silly that could tarnish her parents' reputation. She weighed her each word carefully, and said, "Ashu, I need time. Unlike you, I'm not a bachelor. You understand the complications in the future of our relationship."

He was pragmatic in his expectation, "Yeah, I realize your difficulties. I'm ready to wait. I know you want to spend your life with me in Shimla."

How true he was about her feeling, she thought. She wished he were her husband and she prayed for her wish to come true. After sometime they sneaked into their houses. While she was lucky as her parents were out to their friend's place, he met his mother's anxious gaze as soon as he stepped in.

"You went too far away I guess," she shot her query.

"Yeah, Mummy. I kept driving on."

"So, you enjoyed it."

"Yeah, I did," he spoke hiding his delight.

Though for a moment she felt something was amiss, she brushed it aside. She didn't have to doubt him. He hadn't given her any reasons in the past. Later they had a quiet dinner. When his mother asked him about his return, he told her that he was extending his vacation by another week.

"Hope it's not for me," was her cryptic remark.

"Come on, Mummy," was his mild protest.

And then they retired to their bedrooms. He knew his mother's penchant for cleanliness; hence he removed his clothes and soaked them in the washing machine to get rid off her perfume.

For next few days his life was normal. He met Vaishali twice during the next week and then one day during dinner he dropped the bombshell at the dining table, "Mummy, I'm in love with a girl. I want to marry her."

"Oh, that's great. So who's the lucky damsel? I mean is she from Shimla?" she was ecstatic. Her cheeks glowed in excitement.

He waited for a moment and then spoke, "No, she is a local girl."

"Wow! That's great news, indeed. So, you could find a girl here, after all. What's her name?"

"Vaishali, but Mummy, there's a hitch."

He saw her dimples disappear, her excitement fade away. He didn't know what her reaction would be once he told her everything about Vaishali. But there was no option. He had to tell her some day, then why not today. He gathered courage and spoke, "Mummy, she is married."

"What!" she flung her plate in rage. "Don't tell me you've fallen in love with a married woman. Why? You couldn't find any unmarried girl in the town. It's so disgusting."

"Mummy, please calm down. Mummy please….," he begged.

She moved to and fro in the dining hall fuming with rage. For the first time he had given her a shock, otherwise his behavior until then had been flawless. In the past he had never anguished her by his actions. She was at her wit's end and didn't know how to tackle the storm that threatened to tear their lives apart. And if she didn't stop it, everything which she had built with her hard work would be blown away into pieces.

After divorce from her husband, Ashutosh was all she had in her life. He was more than a son to her. He was her emotional support, her future and the reason to live. Every day she prayed for him and lived for him. She had dreamed for him a well-paying job, a caring and beautiful wife and an excellent future. Without any support from husband, she had raised him single-handedly and hence she had become so attached to him that she wasn't prepared to live without him for a second. So when he moved out to Shimla for his job, she didn't sleep for a week and ate little. She spent her time in crying and thinking about him.

But she didn't want to tell him all that. Instead she tried to reason out with him, "Ashu, I know you don't care for the old values but you have to draw a line somewhere. I'm not against love marriage but I believe you should have the freedom to select the girl you wish to spend your life with."

He thought it prudent to listen to her and hence said nothing.

She resumed, “But I can’t allow this. I mean your marriage to a married woman is out of question. Think, with what face will I meet her parents? If I tell them that I’ve come with the proposal of my son’s marriage with your married daughter, they would throw me out of their house. I won’t blame them. If I were in their shoes I would do the same.”

When she had mellowed down a bit, he argued, “Mummy, I’m not asking you to meet them tomorrow. Let her first seek divorce from her husband and then we can meet her parents.”

“Who’s her husband?” she asked, suppressing anger.

“She’s a sailor’s wife. I mean her husband is an officer in the merchant navy. He’s with the ship in South Africa. He hasn’t come home for the last one year. He doesn’t love her otherwise why would he leave her here for so long.”

“Love, what do you know about love,” she was indignant. “I’m a woman and I know what a lovelorn woman wants from another man when her husband isn’t with her. I won’t embarrass you by asking whether you slept with her but you know what our society thinks of such women.”

“Mummy, please.......,” he protested.

“Ashu, pack your bags and go to Shimla. I won’t like my friends to see you roaming around with that cheap woman.”

He stood up and said, “Mummy, you know me. It’s her or no one. That’s my final decision. Now I leave it to you.”

For several moments she stayed in a state of shock. She knew he was pig-headed but he could be so foolish, she hadn’t visualized. The ground was slipping under her feet, she felt. One wrong move could take her son away from her forever. At the spur of the moment she decided to handle the sensitive issue with tact.

After a few minutes she calmed down and said, “All right, you’ve your way but I’ll talk to her parents when she has taken divorce from her husband.”

He moved closer to her and hugged, “Mummy, you are great. I knew you won’t refuse me. Thank you.”

“Ashu, tell me one thing. Does she love you too?”

“I think she loves me, though she hasn’t admitted yet.”

“OK, then speak to her and gauge her mind. She may not love her husband but that doesn’t mean she loves you. Make sure before moving further. Don’t rush. I won’t like you to suffer the same humiliation and hurt that I suffered after your father left me. Remember, life is too precious to be wasted on someone who doesn’t love you. The world is so big and there are so many wonderful people. There’s always somebody special waiting for you.”

He listened to her. She spoke the words of wisdom, acquired after years of experience. And he knew his mother didn’t want her son to go through the same pain and anguish as she did years ago.

With a node he said, “OK, Mummy. I’ll gauge her mind.”

Later that night they both slept well. He was relieved that his mother had agreed. She was thankful to God for saving her from a catastrophic situation. Now she had some breathing time to think about it.

Despite his best efforts he couldn’t find her for next couple of days and waited for Saturday to meet her in the *sutti*. During their last meeting he had taken her address and phone number but misplaced it. Till Saturday he spent restless hours and thought how to convince her about his love and get to admit that she loved him too. In the intervening period neither he spoke about her, nor did his mother. Their topics for discussion perforce remained mundane like weather, or traffic jams in the city. Traces of rancour between them had diluted much of the warmth in their talks. Each one preferred to keep silent and indulge in least talks.

On Saturday he woke at dawn, put on good clothes and went to the *sutti*. In fact, he was the first buyer to reach there. The vegetables were being unloaded from the trucks. The chill in the air tempted him to have tea. The wait was getting longer. He had begun to harbour doubts about her, whether she would show up at all. If she didn't what would he do, he thought. He was in no position to extend his leave further and if he didn't meet her, he would cut a sorry figure in front of his mother.

His wait lasted a few hours and endless cups of tea before she showed up. This time though he met her straightway. He looked dishevelled and exasperated.

"Hey, Ashu, what's the matter? You look so worked up," she asked.

"Vaishali, I want to discuss something important with you now. Can we go somewhere else?"

"Sure, there's a restaurant close by and this time it's almost empty."

"All right, let's go then. You can buy vegetables later," he said.

The place was empty. They occupied a corner seat and asked for coffee. Without waiting he began, "You know, Vaishali, I've spoken to my mother about our marriage."

"What!" she almost jumped in fright.

"I told her that I'm in love with you and I want to marry you," his voice was filled with excitement.

"What was her reaction?" she asked in fear.

"She was wild and enraged but I was able to convince her. She says that unless you get divorce from your husband she can't talk to your parents about our marriage," he spoke in one breath.

He looked at her. Her calm demeanor surprised him. She looked at him for a while and then said, "Ashu, you are too impatient. I never thought you would rush into this and tell your mother about it. You've jeopardized our relationship. I thought you would wait for sometime before making up your mind about taking me into your life forever. After all, I'm married and I come with complications."

"But I love you, Vaishali," he insisted.

"Hmm."

"Perhaps you don't believe me."

"No, Ashu, it's not that. I do believe you. You are too good a human being to be mine. My destiny isn't that strong. Perhaps I'm not for you. You need someone good, a nice girl to take care of you," she said.

"So, you don't want me as your husband."

"Who said that? I would be a fool to say so but I'm not that lucky. That evening even I had dreamed of marrying you. But my luck has run out."

"Vaishali, but I can't forget you."

"So would I, Ashu."

"Then where's the hitch?"

"You should forget me and our meetings. That's good for both of us," she advised.

"You are speaking my mother's language," he said, raising voice. "Did she meet you? Did she say something to you?"

"How could she? Did you give her my address? How could you when you don't have it yourself," she clarified. "No, she didn't meet me."

"Then."

"My husband's back from South Africa. He is taking me with him from this place. Yesterday night he cried and asked me to forgive him for neglecting me. You see, he made a mistake and deserves a second chance. How can I deny him that," she said, lost in thoughts.

"You made your decision but did you ever think of me," he complained.

"I do feel for you. I always will. In my life you are the first person who made me feel so special, but you'll agree that it's impossible for me to marry you without ruining so many lives. Think about my husband, my parents and your mother. They would be shattered if I took divorce and married you," she looked at him in helplessness. "We can't be selfish. Can we?"

He was speechless. There was substance in her argument. She felt for so many lives. Unlike him, she wasn't selfish. For a moment he felt ashamed of himself. With a guilt-ridden heart he nodded.

"Therefore, we should forget each other and move on in our lives. It's good for both of us. Imagine as if we never met. After all, not everyone's dreams are fulfilled. Millions of people live life based on the compromises and necessities."

"Can you forget me?" he was getting peeved.

"No, but I'll try. Perhaps you don't know that women take longer to come out of any relationship."

"So, where do I go from here?"

"Ashu, don't lose heart. You are a good man and any girl would be lucky to marry you. Perhaps God has made you for someone else and I was trying to steal you from her. He has saved me from committing the sin."

"Vaishali, I don't understand your philosophy. I'm a normal human being with a heart and desires. I find all this weird, strange. I mean whatever you said."

"It's simple. I'll remain a sailor's wife, forever. The resort manager who showed up for a brief period in my life would become a beautiful part of my past that I would safeguard in the innermost depths of my heart. He'll be an eternal source of inspiration to me in the times of distress."

He listened to her in bewilderment, not knowing how to react.

She stood up and said, "I got to go or else my husband would land up here in my search. I've so much to do, buy vegetables, prepare lunch and then do some shopping before leaving this place tomorrow."

"All the best, Vaishali," he said half-heartedly.

She held out her hand for the handshake. As expected, his response was cold. Bitterness, she felt, would help him to forget her soon. With a casual bye she rushed out the restaurant. Outside, he stood still, his eyes followed her every move and watched her enter the melee in the *sutti*. And then he lost her in the crowd forever. For a moment he felt a sharp-pointed knife pierce his heart and give him an excruciating pain.

His eyes searched her among the people moving around that area but he didn't find her. Then he looked for her in the *sutti*. It was same he had seen on the first instance, chaotic, dirty and dusty. The cows, goats and buffaloes intermingled with human beings freely. It was the place where he had found Vaishali and lost her within a span of a few days.

He wondered what his friends in Shimla would think of him if he ever told them about his failed love affair. They would mock at him for falling in love with a married woman in such bizarre circumstances. This incident would remain buried in his heart forever and he would have to endure its pain alone. Its disclosure could make him a laughing stock before his friends.

With heart in his mouth he returned home. It was the longest walk he had ever taken. An anxious mother was waiting for him. Before she could ask, he narrated the entire details of his meeting with Vaishali.

"Her husband has come to take her home," Ashu said in sad tone, as if the sailor was taking Vaishali away against her will.

She gave him a patient hearing and then said, "I'm sorry. Perhaps she wasn't for you. Don't worry Ashu; things will straighten out in due course. With time you would get over this setback."

In the night he spoke to the travel agent and made his reservation plans. Then he announced, "Mummy, I'm going back to Shimla the day after tomorrow."

"OK, *beta*."

On the day of the departure she went to see him off at the railway station. The train was on time and before it was about to leave the station, she hugged him and spoke, "*Beta*, don't worry. God will give you a better soulmate in future. Drop the unpleasant memories here. Start life afresh in Shimla. Find a good girl and marry soon."

"Ji, Mummy," he replied.

She kept waving till the train moved out of sight. With a heavy heart she returned home. At home she opened the drawer of her cupboard and took out a piece of paper, smelling of detergent, that she had found in his Jean's pocket. She unfolded it, spread it on the bed and then picked up the phone. Once she heard someone on the other side, she spoke, "Vaishali, thank you so much. You saved us all. I'll pray for you."

For a while she heard nothing but the usual sobs of a woman, a loser. She replaced the receiver. She looked skywards to ask God why the women had to make sacrifices in relationships, suffer and end up on the losing side.

It was her destiny now to suffer the consequences of failed relationship, she cried.

THE BLUE INK PEN

"Neha, please give me the pen," Samir shouted from the bedroom for his wife who was working in the kitchen.

"Take it from my purse. It's lying there," Neha, who was making dinner, answered.

Samir got up from his table and walked to her cupboard, a meter away. He searched for the pen in her purse, which like any working lady's purse contained a multitude of articles such as a couple of lipsticks of both light and dark shades, a hand mirror, a comb, rubber bands, hair clips, medicines, a small diary, pieces of paper with telephone numbers, and a handcrafted small clutch with money in it.

"Why do women need so many purses for?" he grumbled. And when he didn't find the pen he turned the purse upside down on the bed and emptied it. Still he had no luck. Then he replaced the items in the purse lest Neha caught him. It struck him the pen might be in the cupboard under the clothes, where she often kept things in a hurry. Between the clothes and the plywood lay an ink pen.

Its discovery filled him with a sense of wild joy, which even Archimedes wouldn't have experienced when he had shouted 'Eureka'. With pen in hand, he returned to the table. On a rough piece of paper he checked whether it worked. It didn't. He tried again and again. Still, the result was same.

His joy turned into frustration. Miffed, holding the pen in hand he went to the kitchen and complained, "Neha, It's not working."

"Which one? Show me," she turned back and then yelled, "Why did you take out this ink pen? Didn't I tell you not to touch it? There's a gel pen lying in my purse. You should have taken that."

Stunned by her sudden and uncalled for outburst, he became defensive and apologized, "All right, *baba.* I'm sorry but you don't have to get hyper because I touched this ink pen. Moreover, I haven't written anything with it."

Neha rushed to the bedroom and from her purse took out a gel pen. A speck of dust on the bed caught her attention. A closer look revealed more dust. Handing him the pen she asked, "Samir, did you empty my purse on the bed?"

A lie would have infuriated her further, the truth might bring her temper down; he thought and said with a sheepish grin, "Yeah."

Through her frowned forehead and twitched facial muscles, she smiled and spoke in a gentler tone, "Come on, Samir. I've told you so many times that you should keep the bed clean."

Like a nursery child he nodded. Though it was a mild rebuke from her, it hurt him. He looked back. She was back in the kitchen. Forgetting everything for a while, he started writing important letters to his clients. Engrossed, he forgot about the ink pen but when he finished writing, he recollected her bizarre behaviour and felt hurt. Two years ago, in the first month of their marriage, she had shouted when he had touched the ink pen in jest. He didn't understand then why she was so possessive about it. Two years later, he still searched for the answer of her obsession with a petty, inanimate object.

They ate dinner in silence with Neha doing the talking to mollify him. His contribution in the conversation was a couple of laboured monosyllables. She knew he was upset because of her outburst, but she was confident that he would forget his rancor after sometime. He never kept his anger for long.

After dinner she got busy in winding up the kitchen while he went to bed. And when she entered the bedroom, she found him fast asleep, though he always waited for her. Worried, she shook him, "Honey, I'm sorry for yelling at you," but she got no response. She repeated, "Darling, I'm so sorry." Still, there was no reply. She thought she would apologize to him in the morning. Tired, she fell asleep.

Neha and Samir worked at different places and hence they awoke early to reach office on time. She worked as a consultant and he was an executive in a telecom company. They had well-paying jobs but had to work late hours. They ate lunch at their work places, but had breakfast and dinner at home. On weekends they ate out in the restaurants preceded by a movie in the multiplex.

The couple shared a warm, loving and caring relationship. In third year of marriage they had their share of arguments both on trivial and important issues. But they had shown maturity and respected each other's need for space and privacy. Though with conservative backgrounds, they were progressive in their outlook. A husband and wife relationship is the most complex of all human relations. Lack of knowledge about each other's past likes and dislikes leads to anxiety and puts their bond often under pressure.

Next morning Samir kept silent and after breakfast moved out for the office. Though everyday he dropped her at her office, which fell en route, today he left alone without saying a word to her. She felt he still carried the last night's hurt. A sense of remorse filled her heart. She hired the taxi and went to her office.

The cold war between them lasted a few more days, longer than it had on earlier occasions. But when he resumed talking to her, she found him sulking. Perhaps he needed a few more days, she thought and hence she didn't push him further.

After a fortnight's persistent requests she won him back. They celebrated it with a romantic evening in the famous restaurant. A corner table away from the prying eyes was the perfect setting for a rendezvous. She had put the unsavory incident of the last fortnight behind, while he struggled with traces of the rancor. Sipping soup he bent close to her. She missed a heartbeat in anticipation of those famous words, which a woman loves to hear again and again from her lover.

He whispered, "There's someone you are still fond of."

Waiting to hear 'I love you', she hid her disappointment behind a dry smile. She saw what he was hinting at. Her grin widened, "Yeah, there's someone I love more than you. Do you have any problems?"

"No……no," he fumbled and changed the topic, "Weather is so fine today, perfect for an outing."

Thereafter, they had a quiet dinner. In between, though, they stole glances. She smiled when their eyes met. He, however, kept a serious poise. After dinner he took her for a long drive to rekindle the old passion. Back in the house, they made intense love. She was happy that he had forgotten the unpleasant incident. She had reasons to feel so. Thank God! He got over it; she said to herself and cuddled up to him, who was half-asleep by then.

With passionate night having left by the backdoor, the new dawn didn't bring in the changes she had hoped for. In the morning she found a subtle change in his behavior, which inched towards indifference. In the past he had never felt jealous. Now he did. Often he was lost in his thoughts, ignoring her many times. Despite her best efforts, he sank into the quagmire of suspicion. An impression gained in his troubled heart that the blue ink pen had something to do with her past affair about which she was so touchy. He felt she was hiding something from him.

For three years they had nurtured their marriage with mutual trust and respect. And they had never doubted each other's fidelity or commitment. Both believed that their faith in marriage was unshakable. However, unlike a sensible couple they had forgotten to allow a healthy space between them to exist in which both could treasure their precious past moments and then relive them when they desired. Extreme familiarity had led them to believe that either had a right to an uninterrupted intrusion into other's life.

And too much of spousal interference had often been the cause of distress for both. So, all of a sudden, an inanimate object, a blue ink pen, which had made an abrupt reappearance in their lives, albeit after two years became the cause of friction between them. Though Neha had hidden the pen in her cupboard after that evening's fracas, its image had got imbedded in Samir's mind. While at work, or at the dining table, or in the bathroom, the image of the pen flashed in his mind. He felt the pen mocked at him. A few days later he had a dream that a handsome man gifted that pen to Neha on Valentine's Day in the coffee house, and then both walked, hand in hand, to the waiting car.

From a distance he, in disbelief and disgust, watched her wave at him and then get into the car. He ran behind, shouting, 'Neha, how can you ditch me? You love me. I'm your husband.'

That dream ignited the first spark of jealousy. Samir knew many breakups had happened among his friends because of spousal distrust, but thought of the pen distressed him. A storm brewed up in his heart. He wanted to know the truth about the pen and waited for her to tell him.

When after waiting for months she didn't speak anything about the pen, he became restless and one day, gathering courage, asked, "Neha, is there something about the pen that I need to know?"

"Come on, Samir. Grow up. There's nothing you should lose your sleep over. So, relax," she chided him.

He gave a sheepish smile and left the place. But somehow his heart wasn't ready to accept her clarification that the pen had nothing to do with her past. Perhaps she was hiding her past affair and the pen was a memento from her lover. Otherwise, why would it be so dear to her, a married woman?

After weeks' of brooding he concluded that his wife wasn't going to tell him about the pen and her past affair, and he would have to find the whole thing on his own and then confront her with details. Many questions troubled his mind. Who was the man? Where does he live now? Does she still meet him behind his back? She looked so simple and yet she cheated him with consummate ease, he pondered.

Thought of his wife having an affair repulsed him. He had been faithful and satisfied her every physical and emotional need. Where was the need for her to betray a simple man like him? Consumed with jealousy, he thought of hiring a detective to spy on her.

Next day he walked into a detective agency. The owner welcomed him with a huge smile and offered him tea. From his distraught looks the man knew why he was there. Often the modern marriages were laced with distrust. So, the agency did a brisk business of spying on couples. Regaining poise, Samir said that he suspected his wife was having an affair with her ex-boyfriend and he wanted the detective to find out the truth. A beaming agent explained him the payment plan. The charges were exorbitant but no amount was too big to uncover his wife's wrongdoings, he thought and wrote him a cheque.

The detective advised him, “Sir, please shower your wife with plenty of love and affection, lest she gets suspicious of your motive.”

Then for the next couple of months nothing odd happened. His visits to the detective agency yielded nothing, but false promises. In the meantime the couple willy-nilly allowed the distance between them to widen. She saw something amiss in his unusual display of love and affection, and mood swings. Was it a warning sign of the storm brewing up in their lives? She got worried.

As days passed by their relation became acrimonious. Whatever little love was left between them had long perished. Day by day his behavior deteriorated and he became moody and eccentric. She couldn’t understand why? And she, in utter helplessness, watched him throw dinner plates, cups and other things away in a fit of rage. But for the honour of her parents she would have walked out on him long back. In the hope that some day he would see the reason and repent, she continued to stay with him.

The hell broke loose when one afternoon he landed up with the divorce papers and asked her to sign them. She had dreaded that moment all along, though she wished things hadn’t come to such a pass. An irreversible feeling of gloom gripped her when she saw that the last straw of hope to which she had clung, had given way. It would be both foolish and futile for her, she thought, to remain attached to the sacred thread of marriage that bound them.

She picked up the pen and signed. Then she said, “Samir, please forget what happened between us over the last few months and let’s part on a happy note as friends. I shall leave this house tomorrow. I’ll tell Papa everything. It would be hard for him to accept that his darling daughter has been a failure but………”

The sentence remained unfinished. Her eyes filled up but she didn't cry. In front of him she didn't want to show she was weak and incapable of living alone. Burning with suspicion, he remained unmoved. Instead, he laid the responsibility for the break-up at her doorstep, "I'm not to blame for this sad turn of events. Throughout our marriage I've remained faithful and what do I get in return, a faithless wife."

"Good God! Now you accuse me of infidelity. I should have died before hearing this," she cried in pain.

Someone who had guarded her virginity until marriage, that outrageous accusation tarnishing her character gave her endless anguish. Even in the hurt and humiliation she stayed calm and wondered which of her actions had led him to believe that she was unfaithful to him. With pain in her voice and tears in her eyes, she asked, "Samir, can you tell me when have I cheated on you?"

He blurted out, as if he expected that question, "Oh, don't act so innocent. You pretend to love me with your heart and soul, yet you continued affair with your boyfriend who gifted you that blue ink pen."

For a moment she was speechless. She didn't know whether to laugh or to cry. So, he was the victim of a huge misunderstanding and it was important that she removed the cobwebs in his mind.

Her sobs stopped. She wiped her tears and smiled. It was her first since a long, long time. Then she burst out laughing. Bewildered, he looked at her.

"So, you want to know who gave this blue ink pen to me," she looked at him, "It's my father's. He gifted it to me."

"What!" he exclaimed, in shame.

"Yeah," she resumed, "It was his favourite pen, a Parker with which he wrote many novels that later went on to become the bestsellers. Until he had this pen, his success was modest. You know he is an author. Perhaps it's my fault too. I should have told you about it, but you never showed any interest in his works. Anyway, I was a child then, about six years old, when I first came to know that he was a writer. Since I was his favourite child, among two brothers and a sister, he often took me with him to the market when he went to buy pens, paper and books. One day he asked the stationer for a Chelpark blue ink and a ream of paper. The shop owner advised, 'Sir, time has changed. Nowadays the writers work on the computer. I heard it's much faster and corrections are easier to make. Why don't you also switch over to the computer?' Father, who was unimpressed by his argument, said, 'I'm comfortable with my old typewriter. Maybe tomorrow Neha might use the new machine when she writes.' He then looked at me and ran his fingers through my hair."

She paused to take a breather. His discomfiture had begun to subside.

With pen in her hand, she gazed at it trying to recollect the old memories. A few minutes later she continued, "A year later I went with Papa to the same shop. That was the golden year for the fiction writers in India. In the coffee shops and restaurants the book lovers talked about Arundhati Roy who had the Booker Prize for her book, 'The God of Small Things'. A beaming shopkeeper asked my father, 'Sir, why don't you write in English? One day you will also get a Booker Prize. Then I can flaunt my connection with you.' Papa laughed at his wild idea. After a moment he became serious, 'I can't write in English but I'm sure one day Neha will.' I saw his chest swell with pride by the thought of his daughter writing books. His statement lingered in my mind. Thereafter, I watched his every action in detail and sat beside him when he wrote. I was too young to know what thoughts went on in his mind at that time. He wrote on all days, sometimes in the morning and sometimes in the evening, except on Sundays, which were kept for servicing of his many ink pens. The blue ink pen was his favorite and his superstition too. It was fun to watch his activities on a Sunday morning when he would place a table and a chair in the veranda. Then he would go to the kitchen, boil water in the pan and dip his fingers to feel the temperature. When the water became warm as per his need, he would bring the pan in the veranda and place it on the table. Then he would spread a towel over his lap; keep a clean and dry piece of cloth beside the pan. Dismantling the pen for him was a laborious process. Each item—the nib, the washer, the valve, the cap—was immersed in the warm water and stirred. Thereafter, he would take them out one by one, rinse them, wipe them and blow out the water droplets with his mouth and then reassemble the pens. Later he would fill the ink with a clean dropper. Once the pens were ready he would run them over a rough piece of paper and correct their ink flow by positioning the nib. The hour long exercise made Mummy frown and fret, but he remained unfazed. Even my presence didn't disturb him. I didn't see him pray with so much devotion."

"Why did he gift the pen to you? Has he stopped writing?" Samir asked in a mellowed tone.

"He didn't. In fact, I demanded that he gift it to me. The night before our wedding he came in my room and sat down with me for some time. I saw he was melancholic. My imminent departure from the house had filled his heart with sadness. A perpetual mist had settled in his eyes. After all, his dearest child wouldn't be around him when he would write. I was his inspiration, he told me on many occasions. He wanted to gift me something special, something precious, which would remind me of him. So, he said, 'Neha, I want to give you a costly present. Tell me, if you have anything particular in mind.' He had expected me ask for the car, my childhood ambition but when I said I wanted a thing which was close to his heart, he looked sideways in surprise. He gave up when he failed to guess and urged me to name it. When he heard the blue ink pen, his first reaction was of shock. For several moments he sat dismayed at my choice of gift. And when I told him that I wanted to become a writer like him, he wept. I had never seen him cry like a child before. It gave me a glimpse of the father's love for his daughter. The mothers are known to shed copious tears and express their feeling. There were two reasons for his tears. One, his favorite child, though he never said so in front of the other children, was going away from him. Two, he wanted me to carry forward his legacy of writing. Then he wiped tears, went to his room and came back with his favourite pen. Handing it to me, he said, 'To my lovely daughter and future author.' I was overjoyed. That moment is still so vivid in my mind. He had the satisfied look of a man who had passed on his life's most treasured possession to his most trusted child for safekeeping. His pen is so dear to me that I never wanted to share the sentiments attached to it with anyone, not even you. That explains my bizarre behavior whenever you touched this pen."

He looked at her, she at him. Their eyes welled up. Dithering for a second, he moved closer and hugged her tightly. Their tears rolled down and fell on the broken pieces of the paper, which a moment ago had threatened to rip their lives apart. Neither said a word. They stayed in that position for a long time and let the rancor of the past months flow out. Once their hearts and souls were cleansed thoroughly they separated and gave each other an affectionate look.

"Neha, you should start writing from today itself. Our story won't be a bad idea to begin with," he broke the silence

Holding the pen in her hand, she grinned and nodded.

* * *

Printed by Libri Plureos GmbH in Hamburg, Germany

9 789388 333276